THE BRIGHTSEA SPA KILLER

An enthralling murder mystery with a twist

FRANCES LLOYD

Detective Inspector Jack Dawes Mystery Book 9

Joffe Books, London
www.joffebooks.com

First published in Great Britain in 2022

Cover art by Dee Book Covers

ISBN: 978-1-80405-063-7

PROLOGUE

Mens insana in corpore mortua — an unsound mind in a dead body

It was a warm, pleasant Saturday evening. Detective Inspector Jack Dawes of the Murder Investigation Team and his wife, Corrie, were sitting outside on the patio, enjoying a glass of wine. The atmosphere was relaxed and amicable. All this was about to change.

'Do you realize we haven't had a proper, romantic holiday together since our honeymoon?' observed Corrie.

'Right,' agreed Jack, who was engrossed in the sports page of the *Richington Echo*, and only half listening.

'And we both know what a disaster that was.' She tapped away on her laptop. 'We need a good long break, Jack. That last case really took it out of you. Five harrowing murders in a row and a real battle to nail the killers and find enough evidence to convict them.'

'What took it out of me,' countered Jack, 'wasn't solving the murders. That's what I'm paid to do. It was you interfering and nearly getting yourself drowned.'

She ignored that. 'How much leave have you got owing to you?'

Jack shrugged. 'Dunno — about six weeks, I think. Might be more. Why?'

'I'm booking us some time away. A restful holiday, so we can both unwind.'

Jack put down the paper, sensing something unpleasant was about to happen. 'Corrie, you know I'm not good at holidays. I'm even worse at unwinding. I'm far happier when I'm coiled up like a spring. It's my natural state.'

'Nonsense. Everybody needs a holiday, occasionally. It's for the benefit of your mental and emotional wellbeing, as much as anything.' She was extracting a credit card from her wallet.

Jack started to panic. 'I mean, what exactly are you meant to do on holiday, anyway? It's a toss-up between lying on a beach, among rows of comatose bodies, blistered and burned, like the victims of some mass arson attack. Or you go somewhere bumpy, stagger up a mountain carrying tents, backpacks and dangling mugs, then come back down and recover, in the comfort of your own home. I don't see the point.'

Corrie was resolute. 'It doesn't need to be either of those options. I've found the ideal place. It's a spiritual paradise called the Now to Zen Hotel and Spa. "A glorious combination of timeless elegance and state-of-the-art design, where your body meets your soul." No point arguing, I've already booked us in. Honestly, Jack, it looks awesome online.'

'Siberia looks awesome online. Why is it called the Now to Zen? I thought those places had names like the Moonflower Garden or the Cherry Blossom Temple.'

'You're thinking of takeaways, dear. It's called the Now to Zen because they take you from the state you're in *now* — in your case, stressed and overweight — and transform your mind and body into a state of Zen.'

'What exactly is Zen?' He'd never been absolutely sure.

She pursed her lips, trying to find the words to explain. 'It's, sort of, thinking about not thinking. Persuading your mind to leave stress behind, and focusing on beautiful things that help you relax and feel good about yourself.'

'Clear as mud,' said Jack.

'I'm glad you mentioned mud.' She read from her screen. 'We're going to be "submerged in an oasis of pampering, that lets us leave the pressure of our working lives behind". There are private rooms where we'll have purifying scrubs and massages, followed by mud wraps and seaweed baths. This bit looks good. It says that alongside classical, healthy spa delicacies, the Now to Zen offers its guests exquisite wine and champagne.'

'Corrie, are you sure about this?' He tried desperately to think of an argument that would dissuade her. 'What about Coriander's Cuisine? Who's going to look after that?'

The Cuisine was Corrie's catering business, built up by hard work over many years and it had won several awards. It was her pride and joy. But she wasn't falling for any of Jack's diversion tactics.

'Carlene has been my deputy for a long time. She's confident that she and the team can cope. And no doubt good old Bugsy will get a much-deserved promotion from detective sergeant to acting detective inspector. It's no good, Jack. We're going to do this. And it isn't going to be like our honeymoon on that Greek Island, where you carried on detecting and I took over the catering. This time, I've put down my occupation as "housewife".'

Jack laughed. 'You? A meek little *mouse wife*? That'll be the day.'

Corrie shot him a withering look. 'I've registered you under your real name, Rupert Dawes, and I've put your occupation as electrician.'

He gulped. 'But I don't know anything about electricity. What if they have a power cut? They'll expect me to deal with it.'

'The important thing is, they won't know you're a copper. In the unlikely event that someone gets murdered, they won't expect an electrician to deal with it, will they? And anyway, places like this don't have power cuts. Just look at it.' She turned the screen around so he could see. 'This time next week, we'll be relaxing in a romantic twilight whirl-pool, sipping champagne. No five-course dinners for twenty to prepare and no grisly murders to solve. This is going to be a proper holiday.' She jumped up and capered about. 'We're going to embrace the dandelion! Drink cactus water! Think happy thoughts! What could possibly go wrong?'

CHAPTER ONE

'A holiday, guv?' Detective Sergeant 'Bugsy' Malone was stunned. 'But you never take a holiday. What's brought this on?'

'Corrie,' Jack replied gloomily. 'Apparently we need time to take deep breaths and escape from the stress we've left behind. She says we have to do some "centring" to get back to ourselves and regain our focus. At least, I think that's what she said.'

'Where are you going to do that, sir?' DC Aled Williams was trying to picture the boss being transcendental. It wasn't easy.

'Brightsea. It's a seaside resort on the south coast. Corrie says it's a fusion of cosmopolitan bohemia and whelk stalls.'

'I've been to Brightsea,' said DC 'Mitch' Mitchell. 'We used to take the kids there on holiday when they were little. Now they prefer music festivals and clubbing, and the wife likes a cruise.'

'Corrie's booked us in to a luxury hotel and health spa. It's called the Now to Zen,' added Jack, with little enthusiasm.

'Oh wow! The Now to Zen hotels are absolutely amazing!' enthused DC Gemma Fox. 'They have incredible spas all over the world.'

'You're not kidding.' Clive, the MIT's digital forensics specialist, was reading from the company's website. 'Florida, Marrakesh, Iceland, Thailand, Vancouver Island, Hawaii, to name just a few. Not to mention the usual cities, like London, New York, Paris and Rome. The group is owned by Carter Jefferson III. He must be minted.'

'And he owns the Jefferson beauty brand. They use all those exclusive products in the spas.' Gemma sighed. 'I can't think of anything more luxurious, going from massage to whirlpool to facial. It's my idea of heaven. And wearing a bathrobe all day is actually socially acceptable — encouraged, even.'

'Mrs Parsloe and I spent a weekend in a luxury hotel for our anniversary,' said Sergeant Norman Parsloe, lugubriously. 'In my view, complimentary slippers, a free sewing kit and waking up with a chocolate in your ear, because you didn't notice it on your pillow, hardly justified the astronomical cost.'

'How long do you think you'll be gone, guv?' asked Bugsy.

'As long as it takes to purge my toxins, depressurize my mind and body and unblock my chakras. So, your guess is as good as mine.'

'Sounds more like a job for a plumber to me,' muttered Norman.

'Well, Mrs Dawes has put my occupation as electrician. She doesn't want them to know I'm a copper, in case I get drawn into something stressful.'

'You can see her point,' said Gemma. 'Once folk know you're in the police service, they start asking you to look for their cat or arrest their next-door neighbour for parking in their driveway.'

'I've squared it with the chief super, so as of Monday, Detective Sergeant Malone will be Acting Detective Inspector Malone,' said Jack. 'But don't worry, Bugsy, I'm always at the end of the phone. If something crops up and you need me, I can be straight back here in less than an hour and a half. Don't hesitate to ring me, I shan't mind in the least.'

'Yes, and Mrs Dawes would never forgive me. You go and have a good rest, guv. Forget all about us — the Murder Investigation Team will cope fine.'

'Course we will,' everyone chorused.

Jack smiled bleakly, but his blood was already running cold with dread. This place Corrie had booked was a popular hotel and spa. There would be *people*. While he had no problem interacting with the public in a professional capacity, he always felt awkward having to chat with them socially. What if folk expected him to talk about his job as an electrician? Corrie wouldn't even let him change a light bulb since the time he forgot to turn off the power and stuck his finger in the socket. Never mind a dream holiday, it was shaping up to be his worst nightmare. He'd tried every argument he could think of to talk Corrie out of it, including the astronomical cost, but she was resolute. There would be no pseudo-mystical, hippy nonsense, she promised him, just self-love and pampering, in a beautiful environment.

* * *

It was the society wedding of the year. Abigail 'Abbie' Jefferson, sole heiress to the Jefferson empire, was marrying Antonio 'Toni' Di Vincenzo, son of an Italian count. The entire three-day affair was nothing short of fabulous. It was hosted by the flagship Now to Zen Hotel and Spa, on a hill in California, overlooking the Pacific Ocean. The Jefferson estate owned some hundred acres, along the central Californian coastline.

Guests included a bunch of Hollywood A-listers and icons from the world of fashion and beauty, who took full advantage of the facilities during their stay. They dined on lobster and caviar and all the champagne they could drink, often diving into the aqua-blue oasis pool while wearing thousands of dollars' worth of finery.

Abbie looked breath-taking. She wore no fewer than six different wedding dresses throughout the various stages of her nuptials, while the handsome Antonio played it cool in a Dolce & Gabbana velvet tuxedo. Their images had been perfectly reproduced in fondant icing atop the elaborate five-tier wedding cake. The honeymoon was to be a world tour of the Now to Zen hotels, starting in the UK and Brightsea on the south coast of England. While it was not, by any means, as lavish as the London spa, it was especially attractive to Abbie. She found the sight and sound of the Channel very 'English', not to say 'European'. She planned to walk barefoot on the sand at midnight with her gorgeous new husband.

The epic, three-day wedding celebration followed by the journey from California to Brightsea had been exhausting. Abbie and Toni relaxed in style in a private spa suite, set aside for the most affluent guests. It had been designed using cool azure marble, juxtaposed with classic white alabaster columns.

Abbie gazed adoringly at Toni across the twilight whirlpool. 'Are you happy to be in England, honey?'

He took her hand and kissed it. '*Si, mia cara moglie.* I am happy anywhere, as long as I'm with you.'

She loved his Italian accent. It had been one of the things that had attracted her when they first met at a party in Los Angeles. That, and the fact that he was the son of a count, even if it was only a courtesy title. And, of course, he was impossibly handsome.

She kissed him on the cheek. 'We'll spend a few days here, then we'll fly to Monaco and you can play the tables in Monte. You know how much you love gambling. Daddy has taken care of the private jet and all the financial arrangements. It will be just great, Tonino.'

He lifted the champagne bottle out of the ice bucket at the side of the pool and topped up her glass. 'Where shall we live when the honeymoon is over? I don't think it should be in the UK.'

She floated across into his arms. 'Anywhere you like. Shall we buy a villa in Italy? Tuscany is so beautiful. Florence, Pisa, Siena, Lucca — you choose, honey.'

He hesitated. 'Maybe not Italy. I am not in favour with the Mafiosi right now. I shouldn't want the paparazzi looking into my activities and exposing me to my enemies.'

'Oh yeah, Daddy told me. Well, they won't dare harm you now that you're under the protection of Carter Jefferson III.' She put her arms around him and he kissed her, long and passionately, while the blue water swirled about them. She thought she must be the luckiest woman alive.

* * *

The semi-detached house of Fred and Rita Withenshaw, on the corner of Ribble Street in Clitheroe, was unremarkable. The bay windows and the stained-glass panel in the front door were typical of houses built in the fifties. On a normal day, the garden was tidy, the tiny patch of grass mowed and the flower beds free from weeds. But this was not a normal day — this was Fred and Rita's ruby wedding anniversary, and the small house was overflowing with guests, helping them to celebrate. Their four children had gone to town with the decorations. Ruby banners and balloons adorned every space, inside and out. At teatime, there were ham baps, vol-au-vents, pork pies and a red velvet anniversary cake. They drank a Lambrusco toast — Rita's favourite — to forty years of wedded bliss, then their eldest daughter presented them with the gift that was from everyone, friends and family.

'Mam, Dad, we all chipped in for this present. We hope you like it.' She handed over a large envelope.

'Whatever can it be?' Rita wondered. She tore it open with some trepidation and put on her glasses to read the document inside. It was a brochure accompanied by a holiday voucher for two at the Now to Zen Hotel and Spa in Brightsea.

'What is it, Mother?' asked Fred.

'It's a holiday, Dad,' replied Rita. 'We're to get the train to London, then there's a coach to take us to a luxury hotel. Look at the pictures. It's beautiful. We get all sorts of treatments and we can sit in bubble baths and lie on a couch to be massaged.'

'Good. Happen it'll ease my rheumatism, it's been playing up something chronic since the weather changed.' Given a choice, he'd have preferred one of those chairs that go up your staircase, rather than a fancy holiday.

Rita looked at her children, who were watching her with anxious expressions, hoping she was pleased. 'Thank you so much. It's a wonderful present. We've never had the chance to do anything like this before. Our holidays, when you were all young, were spent walking on Morecambe Beach, Dad with his trousers rolled up and me carrying the picnic and the buckets and spades. It will be such a treat to be waited on and not have to cook and wash up.'

That night, Fred and Rita went to bed exhausted from all the excitement. Fred reached across to set the alarm, a habit he did every night, even though they were both retired. 'Well, what do you reckon to that, Mother? You and me having a holiday in a posh hotel. Will I like it, d'you think?'

'You can suit yourself, but I'm going to enjoy it.' She was thumbing through the glossy brochure. 'There hasn't been much luxury in my life, what with bringing up four kids and working as a dinner lady for nigh on thirty years. I'm going to squeeze every ounce of pleasure from my holiday in this health spa. And you can mind your manners, too. No cutting your toenails on the carpet or breaking wind in the lift. And the beds are all super -king-size, so I won't have to listen to you snoring in my ear every night.' She picked up a notebook from the bedside table, where she was making a list, prior to the big event. 'I'll need to get you some new swimming trunks. Your old ones have got holes in the bum and I'm not having you sitting there bare arsed in the twilight whirlpools. Whatever would people think?'

CHAPTER TWO

David stared at his computer screen and frowned. There it was again — for the fifth time. As the senior UK software engineer for the major tech company owned by Carter Jefferson III, he spent most days knee-deep in the Now to Zen databases, checking for anything irregular. One day, he happened across a piece of malicious code, designed to steal financial information from one of the spas. He had reported it and deleted it. Some time later, he came across that same code again, but this time, it was in the database of a completely different Now to Zen spa. Over the last few weeks, he had found it again and again, in several others. He decided messaging wasn't immediate enough, so he telephoned the Jefferson US IT manager and explained his concerns.

'There's something dodgy going on, boss. What do you want me to do?'

'Where did you first spot this malicious code? Which of the spa databases?'

'It was the one in Brightsea. It seems to have spread from there.'

'Well, Dave, I guess you're the best person to figure out who's planting it. I want you to go undercover. Book yourself into the Brightsea Now to Zen — the business will cover the cost. Some crook is helping himself to the company's cash. Find out who it is and report back. Don't trust anyone. From the techniques you describe, they're smart, these guys, and they won't hesitate to shut you down. Have you got that?'

'Yes, boss.'

If asked to describe himself, David would have said he was socially inept. While he had no problem with technology, however complex, he had severe difficulties with people, especially in a confrontational situation. When he found out who was cooking the books, he imagined it would become extremely confrontational.

He went home to his bedsit to pack and to ring his mother to tell her he wouldn't be around for a week or two. If he was brutally honest, he relished a few weeks free from his mother's constant surveillance. It was one of the reasons why he'd never had a proper girlfriend.

* * *

'Eddie, I know you're there. Pick up or I'll come round and nail your balls to the front door of your fancy apartment.'

Damn! Eddie 'Coke' Clayton cursed silently. *How the hell did she find me?* Reluctantly, he picked up the phone, knowing she was quite capable of carrying out her threat, if he didn't. 'Hello, Della. How lovely to hear from you.'

'No, it isn't. It's your worst nightmare and you know it. I guess you thought I was finished, after you bailed out and left me. Well, I'm back and I want money. After everything that's happened, I think you owe me, don't you?'

'I'd love to help, sweetheart, but I'm undergoing a period of financial embarrassment myself, as it happens. Leave me your number and I'll contact you when I'm back in funds.'

'The hell you will. You don't get to take a rain check this time. Do you seriously believe I learned nothing from the years we were married? You must have made a fortune from that last drug heist before you took a hike and left me to take the heat. Now, I want my share. Otherwise, our mutual friends might find out your new name and where you're holed up. We both know you wouldn't last long after that. And you screwed up big time when you shot that cop — you're damn lucky he didn't die.'

Eddie thought quickly. She was right, of course. If the organization found him, he'd end up in the Thames wearing concrete boots. It was either that or inside a pillar supporting a motorway flyover. They'd done both to men who'd double-crossed them in the past. And they'd want their money back. If the filth got him, it would hardly be much better. He'd wounded a copper — one of their own. He wouldn't see the light of day until he was a pensioner, at least. 'All right. How much do you need?'

'Fifty grand. There's something I have to do and I need cash — lots of it.'

'What do you have to do that's so important you'd come crawling out from under a rock and harass me for it?'

'Not that it's any of your goddam business, but I've decided to go back and live in the States. Just get me the cash.'

'Tell me where you are, and I'll bring it.' He had no intention of doing anything of the kind, but he had to buy some time.

'Oh no, you don't. I'll meet you.' She gave him details of the time and place. 'Make sure you bring the cash or I'll jack up the price.' She looked again at the pictures on the cover of the high-end lifestyle magazine that had prompted her urgent call.

After he'd put down the phone, Eddie was deep in thought. Why would the stupid cow want to meet there, of all places? Three single malts later, he'd worked out a way to get himself off the hook. It was risky, but what choice did he have? If she'd been able to track him down, how long before others would? He wouldn't put it past her to have tipped off the organization already. He needed to get out of there and fast. He opened a drawer in his desk and took out a gun.

* * *

13

Peggy and Dorothy Buncombe were sisters, only two years apart in age, but in looks and personality, they were chalk and cheese. Together, they ran the Happy Horses Riding Stables, deep in the heart of rural Somerset. Peggy was muscular, ruddy-faced and permanently wind-swept from a lifetime spent mostly outdoors, in all weathers. A confirmed spinster, she regarded men as useful only when the stables needed mucking out or the drains were blocked. Dorothy, the younger sister, was slim, fashion-conscious and permanently on the lookout for attractive male company. In her immediate vicinity, they were few and far between. She had tried and discounted the hearty farmers, who smelled of livestock, and the cider makers, with their bibulous noses.

Even the sisters' riding preferences were different. Peggy favoured vigorous cross-country rides, requiring both horse and rider to be in excellent physical shape, and to be brave and trusting of each other. Peggy fitted this description perfectly. Mounted on her horse, Saracen, she conquered stone walls, streams, ditches and fences with consummate ease, despite the fact she was no longer as young and fit as she used to be.

Dorothy preferred dressage. She enjoyed the challenge of balance, rhythm and suppleness, and most importantly, the obedience of her horse and its harmony with her as rider. Her Arab mare, Concubine, was a perfect foil for Dorothy's temperament. And she could still turn heads among the horsey community in her short jacket, white breeches and top hat. It had been mainly her suggestion that they needed a couple of weeks of rest and recuperation. Peggy had been thrown, during a particularly gruelling ride and without a crash vest, and her back was giving her problems. Dorothy had seen a brochure for the Now to Zen in the hairdresser's and decided it would be just the place to hook up with a handsome, rich, romantic interest with a view to — well, anything she fancied, really. And she guessed there would be physios there, to sort out Peggy's back.

They had just finished feeding and watering for the last time before the stable hands took over.

'I'm really looking forward to this holiday, aren't you, Peggy?'

'They say the South Downs are a good hack.' Peggy heaved a net of hay over the wall with one arm. 'The chalk downland provides good going, even after rain, I'm told.'

'Peggy, we're not taking Saracen with us,' Dorothy chided.

'I know, but I expect we could hire a couple of decent mounts while we're there.'

'I'm not going to a very expensive and luxurious health spa just to do what I do every day at home,' declared Dorothy, firmly. 'I'm hoping to find a male companion.'

Peggy looked her sister up and down. She had mud on her face, muck on her boots and she was wearing baggy old jodhpurs and an ancient hacking jacket. She scoffed. 'You won't get a man dressed like that, Dotty.'

'I don't want a man dressed like this. I want one dressed like James Bond, in a white dinner jacket with a red carnation in his buttonhole. Preferably not with a gun down his trousers, though. I know your preference is to spend your holiday with a big, hard gelding between your thighs, but I have other ideas.'

'Dorothy! Really!'

* * *

'Mr and Mrs Bennett?' The door opened and the couple relationship counsellor poked her head out. 'Would you like to come through?'

Timothy Bennett reckoned the young woman looked about twelve. What could she know about anything? Reluctantly, he stood up, wondering why he was wasting time here, when he could be down the pub with his mates. His wife, Miriam, put a firm hand on the small of his back and propelled him through the door into the consulting room. They sat in comfortable chairs around a small, circular table. On the top, there was a box of tissues and a pile of inspirational leaflets. Tim noticed the top one was entitled, *Marriage – Why did you sign up to it?*

Good question, Timothy thought. It was around twenty years ago, and he didn't remember much, only that he'd been drunk and it had seemed like a good idea at the time. He recalled buying a motorbike under similar circumstances, although the long-term consequences were somewhat different. You could always sell a motorbike when you got fed up with it.

'My name's Sally.' The counsellor smiled insipidly. 'How can I help?'

That was exactly what Tim was wondering. This psycho-bollocks was costing him money, so he decided to buy into it. 'My wife needs to learn to stop nagging.'

Miriam bridled, as she did almost every time Timothy opened his mouth. 'Don't listen to him, he doesn't know what he's talking about. Ask me about his filthy lavatory habits, the disgusting noise he makes when he's eating and the rotting food left behind in that grimy beard. Then there's the state of his underpants after . . .'

Sally blanched. 'Could we perhaps discuss some less . . . er . . . intimate issues. For example, who is the more critical of the other's behaviour?'

'He is.'

'She is.'

The response was simultaneously vociferous.

'Right . . . How about emotional validation? By that, I mean having your partner hear what you're saying, appreciate you and understand you.'

'That would only work if Mim stopped nagging long enough to listen,' said Tim.

'I'd listen if Tim ever said anything worth listening to,' Mim fired back.

Tim leaned towards Sally. 'Tell me, love, are you married?'

'Er . . . no, as a matter of fact, I'm not,' she said, embarrassed.

'I didn't think so, or you wouldn't be asking such bloody silly questions.'

Sally ploughed on valiantly. 'When I talk to couples about their relationship, I find, more often than not, that it's the little things that carry a lot of weight. One short and sweet text or email a day can make your lover's heart go pitter-patter.'

Miriam snorted. 'Oh, he does that. I've seen them on his phone. He sends them to the barmaid at the Nag's Head.'

'Where the hell did that one bloody come from?' Tim was shocked. 'How did you get into my phone, you nosey cow?'

'And if we're talking about "little things", he's got one of those, all right.' She laughed, unpleasantly. 'Ask the barmaid at the Nag's Head.'

Tim retreated into stonewalling mode. He sat back in his chair, arms resolutely crossed and legs manspread, in a sub-liminal power pose, to show that, literally and figuratively, he still had balls. Sally sighed to herself. Two more candidates for soul-nourishing activities. Her cousin, Penny Hawkins, together with husband, Richard, managed the Now to Zen Hotel and Spa in Brightsea, just along the coast.

'Now, in situations such as this, my advice would be to spend some quality time together. Make time for date nights in romantic surroundings. Seek an opportunity for some undisturbed fun time.' She winked, archly, and pulled a Now to Zen brochure from the bottom of the pile on the table. 'I'd recommend at least a couple of weeks here. It's worked wonders for so many of my couples.'

Tim left wondering what would be the benefit of con-tinuing their conflict, in different, hugely expensive sur-roundings, barely a few miles from where they lived. But Mim decided they should give it a go.

Sally telephoned her cousin. 'Penny? Two more for you. He's an obnoxious arse with unpleasant personal hab-its and she's a spiteful bitch with a vicious tongue. Usual commission?'

CHAPTER THREE

Penny Hawkins stood at the front desk, waiting to review the list of new arrivals. Meredith, the hotel receptionist, had booked in some of them on the computer herself, but some of them had registered themselves online, like an increasingly large number of their guests. It saved hanging about, filling in lots of forms, and they could state their problems and requirements without any embarrassment. As managers of the Brightsea Now to Zen, Penny and Richard took a keen interest in the guests, their backgrounds and their individual requests. Penny would then design a programme of treatments that best suited their needs. When they were ready to leave, the computer would work out their bill, which was almost always colossal, and they paid with their recorded credit card.

'Who do we have this week, Meredith?'

'They're a right mixed bunch, Mrs Hawkins.' Meredith passed her a printout of their names and details. 'There's Mr and Mrs Dawes, a nice couple, although he doesn't say much. She's a housewife, he's an electrician. They're here to de-stress and lose weight, according to their registration form.'

Penny's brow creased. 'I'm not sure people can do both at the same time. In my experience, a combo of starvation and exercise usually increases the stress, but I expect I can design something suitable involving champagne. Not too many calories, and after the first bottle they'll soon forget they're stressed and chubby.'

'Mr and Mrs Withenshaw have travelled all the way down from Lancashire by train and coach. They're here to celebrate their ruby wedding. It was a present from their friends and family. They went straight to their room so Mr Withenshaw could soak his feet and Mrs Withenshaw could have a cup of tea.'

'Make sure the kitchen knows it's their anniversary. Chef will design a cake.'

Meredith frowned. 'Mr and Mrs Bennett, "Tim and Mim", were referred here by your cousin, following relationship counselling.'

'Oh yes. How are they getting on?'

'First off, she called him a penny-pinching pig because he didn't tip the valet who parked their car. He replied that if her brain was as big as her gob, she'd have read in the online brochure that gratuities were included in the massively inflated tariff.'

'Cheek!' said Penny. 'This is a top-of-the-range hotel and spa, not a budget-price hostelry. Mrs Bennett's right — he is a penny-pinching pig. How are the Buncombe sisters settling in?'

'Well, the older lady, Peggy, with the awful complexion, either needs urgent professional attention or she needs to wear a bag over her head, to protect her face from the ravages of the weather. She asked where she could hire a horse, as she wants to hack on the Downs. The younger one, Dorothy, spotted Louis working out in the gym and said, "Book me in for whatever it is he does."'

'Louis is very popular with our more mature lady guests,' observed Penny.

'He's very popular with ladies of all ages.'

Louis, the sports and exercise trainer, had abs and pecs most young men would die for. He was much in demand for tennis coaching, keep-fit classes, rounds of golf, swimming lessons and various other physical activities, not necessarily on the spa's syllabus.

'Speaking of gentlemen who are popular with the ladies, is Sir Marcus Wellbeloved having a relaxing time? Such a gentleman — beautiful manners and so well educated. He's booked himself in for lots of therapies.'

'Yes, I think he's working his way through the whole programme — and the wine list. His bill will be enormous when he leaves. How long is he staying?'

'He didn't say. Now, remember, Meredith, we don't mention money at Now to Zen, especially with regard to Sir Marcus. I have absolutely no doubt at all that he'll be able to settle his account, no matter how substantial. The important thing is that the guests are made to feel physically pampered, mentally refreshed and that they have achieved whatever it was they thought they'd come here to do.'

'Yes, Mrs Hawkins. But it doesn't seem to be working with David — the young man who booked in with social anxiety. We hardly see him.'

'That's because he's socially anxious,' said Penny. 'He needs a spiritual advisor. I'll book him some sessions with Rainbow. She'll read his aura and guide him to better overall health.'

'We don't see much of the honeymooners in the private bridal suite, either,' observed Meredith.

'We don't need to. Just having Count Antonio and Abigail Jefferson-Di Vincenzo staying here is a feather in our cap. It's a pity we can't advertise it more widely, but the order came down from above that the couple wanted to stay out of the press now that the wedding's over. They just want to chill out.'

Meredith sighed. 'They'll be off around the world soon. Do you think the rumours about the Mafia being after him are true?'

'No, of course not. He's Italian nobility. He wouldn't be involved in anything criminal. And now he's the son-in-law of

Carter Jefferson, so that makes him above suspicion as far as the Now to Zen Corporation is concerned — and that includes us.'

* * *

Corrie and Jack had unpacked and were relaxing on the balcony of their deluxe room, enjoying a glass of champagne and a glorious view of the coast. At least, Corrie was enjoying it. She took a deep breath of sea air.

'Isn't this wonderful, Jack? Aren't you glad you came?'

'I'll let you know after we get back home. Experiences like this are always judged more accurately with hindsight, and the realism hits when you've seen the bill.'

'I hope you aren't going to be like this for the entire holiday.'

'Like what?'

'A cross between Scrooge and Eeyore. I'm planning to enjoy every minute and you won't put me off, however much of a misery you intend to be.'

'I don't intend to be a misery, sweetheart, it's just that I don't know what to do on holiday. It's all so haphazard and unstructured.'

'That's what holidays are supposed to be like. You just hang out and chill. Carlene said so. And anyway, it isn't that unstructured. Penny Hawkins has drawn up a schedule of events for us.'

He looked at his watch. 'OK, so what does this schedule say we should do now?'

Corrie looked at it. 'We go down to dinner.'

'Good. At least that makes sense. I'm starving.'

'There are three dining rooms. I wonder which one we should use.' While Corrie was pondering, there was a tap on the door. She opened it to an attractive young lady wearing black trousers and a black tunic bearing the Now to Zen logo and carrying a clipboard.

'Hello, Rupert and Coriander. I'm Kelly-Anne, your spa buddy. It's my job to guide you through the range of

21

speciality treatments that have been designed *pacifically* for you, that is, by way of a special *itinerinerary* of massages, facials and hydrotherapy, as well as beauty services and special exercises. I don't do the spiritual stuff, though. You get a different Zen buddy for that.'

Corrie could tell she had learned her script off by heart and presumably trotted it out to every new guest on their first day. 'If we're going to be buddies, do you think you could start by calling us Jack and Corrie?'

Kelly-Anne looked doubtful. She consulted her clipboard again. 'I'm not sure. It says "Rupert and Coriander" on my *calendrier des rencontres.*'

Corrie was amused at her French pronunciation, which was basically English. 'All the same, I think you'll find Jack and Corrie easier.'

She still looked bewildered but capitulated. The guest was always right. 'It's half past seven, so I'm guessing you're freakin' famished. Dinner is a speciality feature of the Now to Zen, with every meal . . . er . . . specially cooked.'

Corrie smiled. 'Yes, we are hungry. We were wondering which of the three dining rooms we should use.'

'Well, I can help you there, Jack and Corrie. The Dorchester Room is dead smart. You have to wear evening dress — that means a posh frock for you, Corrie, and a dinner jacket and dicky bow for you, Jack. There's proper silver service — that's service with . . . er . . . proper silver servers, and a bloke who plays the piano while you eat. Or you might prefer the Ritz Restaurant.' She studied her clipboard once more. 'It's cool and refreshing, scented with floral bouquets and there's serene, melodious birdsong instead of a piano. It doesn't matter what you wear, but no shorts, T-shirts, jeans, flip-flops, hoodies, string vests or swimwear, which is a pity because I look dead fabulous in a bikini.' She went off-piste to explain. 'This isn't my real job, you see. I'm a glamour model and reality star, I just do this in between engagements. You've probably seen me on the TV as Kelly-Anne Destiny. I was a competitor in *The Great British Paperhanger.*'

Jack was fascinated but not in a good way. 'Did you win?'

'Oh, I didn't hang any actual wallpaper. I just stood there in these really cute overalls and pointed to a bucket of paste. Then the camera cut to someone less gorgeous than me, obvs—'

'Obvs,' confirmed Corrie.

'—but who knew how to do it,' finished Kelly-Anne.

'Knew how to do what?' Jack was rapidly losing the thread of this conversation.

'You know . . . stick it to the wall . . . the paper.'

'But why would you want to do that?' asked Jack.

Kelly-Anne looked at him, pityingly. 'The money's good and I got to keep the overalls. But I'm trying to lose weight while I'm here.'

Corrie looked at her, thinking she must be a size eight at most.

'My agent says I'll end up demonstrating tea towels if I don't recapture my runaway midriff.'

'What's the third dining room called?' asked Jack, stomach rumbling.

'We call it the Cheerful Chophouse. It's for people who can't be arsed to change out of their bathrobe and complimentary slippers. No piano or birdsong, just the noise of the other diners chewing. The steak and chips are good, though.'

'We'll go there,' said Jack immediately.

'No, we won't. We'll get dressed up and try the Dorchester Room, tonight.' Corrie brooked no argument.

'Good choice,' said Kelly-Anne. 'I'll book you in.'

Jack wondered, rather uncharitably, if she got commission from persuading guests to take the expensive option.

'Now, when you've finished your meal, I'll be waiting to escort you to a pod in our twilight whirlpool chamber. It's a chamber with . . . er . . . pods of twilight whirlpools and it's the perfect way to end the evening, relaxing in fizzy blue water. Although, I should *hallucinate* for your *condemnation*, it's not the actual water that's blue, it's just blue light bulbs under the water. They make it blue. See you later.'

After she'd gone, Jack asked, 'Why did you say we'd eat in the posh dining room? I'd have been perfectly happy with a steak in the Cheerful Chophouse.'

'I know you would, but I'm interested to see how good the food is here.'

Jack groaned. 'Corrie, promise me you won't ask to see the chef and complain his chateaubriand is overcooked or the halibut's still got bones in it, like you have in all the other restaurants we've visited.'

She grinned. 'You can take the chef out of the Cuisine but you can't take the Cuisine out of the chef. Come on, get your glad rags on or we'll be late.'

CHAPTER FOUR

The ambience in the Dorchester Room was one of understated wealth. Diamonds twinkled in the soft mood lighting as heavily ringed hands reached for another glass of Dom Pérignon. A dress-suited pianist coaxed discreet Ivor Novello from the keys of the white grand piano, a subtle background to the prandial hum of conversation.

'This is the life, isn't it, darling?' Corrie had shoehorned herself into her only evening dress. It was an unassuming wrap-over creation with a tie belt. She looked around at all the sequinned haute couture and hoped she didn't get mistaken for the cleaning lady.

Jack ran a finger around the inside of his dress collar. He reckoned it had somehow shrunk since he'd last worn it, as it seemed to be trying to throttle him. He wondered if he'd still be able to swallow when the food arrived. 'Yes, this is the . . . er . . . life, but I'm not sure I'd want to do it every night.'

Corrie glanced surreptitiously at the other diners. On the next table, a suave, well-groomed man in his forties nodded to her and smiled. She smiled back.

He leaned across. 'Good evening. I'm Sir Marcus Wellbeloved.'

'Pleased to meet you. I'm Corrie Dawes.'

'Corridors?'

His quizzical response was the same she'd heard a million times before, when she told people her name. 'It's a long story.' Unsure of what to say next, Corrie blurted out, 'Do you come here often?' Then she felt foolish.

'No, this is the first time. How about you?'

'Jack and I are here to unwind. He's an electrician, aren't you, darling?'

Jack looked up from the menu. 'Er . . . yes, that's right. It can be very stressful, all those different coloured wires and diagrams and um . . . fuse boxes and things.'

Sir Marcus raised his eyebrows but didn't comment. He knew a copper when he saw one. Why the alter ego? He smiled and returned to his lobster and champagne.

Across the room, Fred and Rita were examining the menu while a patient waitress stood by.

'Do I like lobster thermidor, Mother?' Fred asked. His dinner jacket had wide, notched lapels and smelled faintly of mothballs.

'Yes.' Her taffeta skirts rustled when she moved.

'Am I having that, then?'

'No.' She positioned her glasses on top of her head and looked up at the waitress. 'He would if I let him. He'd wolf it down, no bother, if I didn't stop him. It's the same with prawn vindaloo. Next thing, he'd be stretched out on the bathroom floor like a draught excluder, face all red and lumpy, throat swelling up and gasping for breath. He can't stomach crustaceans, he's allergic.' She examined the menu. 'He'll have haddock, chips and mushy peas. *I'll* have the lobster thermidor.'

When Jack's meal arrived, he peered at it suspiciously. 'Corrie, listen to this.' He read out the description on the rather pretentious menu.

A flank of Sussex beef from the historic High Weald breed is marinated for three days then simmered in wine. It is then shredded into strands and lubricated with a confit of shallots, thinly sliced and caramelized to add sweetness. Locally grown potatoes are cubed, cooked

26

sous vide, and carefully combined with the sautéed beef. Tender haricot beans, baked in a tomato-infused sauce, are served alongside. Chef recommends the addition of a dash of his speciality Now to Zen piquant sauce, a perfectly balanced blend of molasses, dates, apples, tamarind and spices.

'You're the food expert, but that sounds to me like corned beef hash, baked beans and brown sauce.'

Corrie laughed. 'That's exactly what it is, but it sounds good, doesn't it? Fair play to whoever writes the menu.'

Timothy and Miriam had started the evening on an uneasy truce. Mim had dressed up for dinner and believed she looked glamorous until Tim told her that her pale, skinny body and pink frizzy hair made her look like a stick of Brightsea candyfloss. She hit back by telling him that the noise he made sucking asparagus was like listening to a cow trying to pull its foot out of the mud, whereupon he stood up and shouted, so everybody heard, that he was going to find some attractive company in the seafront nightclubs. Then he stormed out and left Miriam sitting there.

There was an uncomfortable silence while everybody pretended not to notice. Even the pianist stopped playing. It was so quiet Corrie could hear the bubbles popping in Sir Marcus's champagne on the next table.

* * *

The Buncombe sisters had opted for the Cheerful Chophouse. Peggy didn't understand the concept of fine dining. In her view, eating was something you did in order to gain the energy for a 'bloody good gallop' on the heath. You got the meal over as quickly as possible — sometimes, without even bothering to sit down — and you certainly didn't get done up 'like a dog's dinner' to eat it. Added to which, she didn't possess any garments with a skirt. Dorothy was disappointed as she didn't imagine she'd meet any James Bond lookalikes in what amounted to little more than a café. She'd hoped to form a closer acquaintance with the dashing Sir Marcus. But she changed her mind when she discovered the staff used it. When Louis came in at ten o'clock for a late-night burger, he'd winked at her as he passed her table. She'd put her name down for his 'Stay Young and Beautiful' exercise classes.

Since his arrival, David had been hard at work, attempting to discover the source of the malicious code emanating from this branch of the Now to Zen Group. So far he'd drawn a blank, but he had several more links to follow up. Feeling hungry, he realized that it was too late for a meal in any of the dining rooms, so he'd contacted room service, ordered a panini and a pot of coffee and carried on working.

In the private suite of Abbie and Toni Jefferson-Di Vincenzo, the couple had enjoyed their usual luxury in-room dining experience with oysters, caviar, venison and champagne delivered on trolleys by an entourage of dining staff. After they'd eaten, Abbie had donned her customary earplugs and sleep mask and fallen asleep on the massive circular bed. Still fully clothed, Toni stood outside on the balcony, watching the sea fret drifting in. He downed his third straight bourbon and wondered what to do next. Why the hell had he agreed to start the honeymoon in a dump like Brightsea? He should have insisted on flying straight to Monaco. Too late now. But if he panicked, it could all go horribly wrong. He must keep his nerve. There was too much to lose.

* * *

Jack and Corrie finished their meal just before midnight. They were pretty much the last diners to leave. Mercifully, Corrie could find nothing wrong with her filet mignon and baby vegetables, but she couldn't help thinking that a peashoot garnish would have improved the presentation. She had allowed Jack to eat his corned beef hash without criticism.

Jack half-hoped Kelly-Anne might have forgotten about them and gone to bed. All he wanted to do was get out of this uncomfortable monkey suit and into his pyjamas. But Kelly-Anne had other ideas. Her clipboard said Mr and Mrs Dawes were to have a twilight whirlpool experience and it was her job to make sure it happened, no matter how late. She caught up with them as they were leaving the Dorchester Room.

'Come along now, Jack and Corrie, let's get you into your swimsuits and bathrobes, then I'll leave you to *medicate* in your special pod.'

Suitably garbed, they trooped down to what was now a midnight, rather than twilight, whirlpool chamber, which seemed to Corrie more spooky than romantic.

Feeling a trifle awkward, Jack muttered to Corrie, 'Do we have to do this? It's gone midnight. Can't we just say we're tired and we'll do it another time?' Much later, he was to remember this feeling and decided it would have been a valuable premonition, had he chosen to listen to it.

'Certainly not.' Corrie was determined they should 'embrace the dandelion' at every opportunity. If that meant extraordinary experiences at unaccustomed times, then that was exactly what they'd come to do.

They turned a corner to find the secluded whirlpool, hidden between curved blue marble partitions. At first glance, it seemed a haven of tranquillity, designed to calm the senses at the end of the day and prepare the body and mind for sleep.

'This is your pod.' Kelly-Anne stopped. 'Oh dear. This isn't right. There's somebody in there already.' She approached officiously. 'Excuse me, madam, but you're in the wrong whirlpool.'

They could just make out a figure in the gloom. She was slumped over in the pool, leaning against the side and not moving.

'Madam, you have to wake up. You shouldn't be in here. My clipboard says Jack and Corrie Dawes are supposed to—' She went nearer then gasped. 'Oh my god! Her eyes are open and her face is all twisted. I think she's ill.' She bent down and reached to take the woman by the arm.

'Don't touch her!' Jack shouted. Startled, Kelly-Anne jumped back, which, as the coroner would say later, probably saved her life. 'I think she's been electrocuted.' Jack was sure of it. The blue lights around the edge of the pool and under the water were flickering and the water was no longer swirling. 'We must all move right away. Don't touch anything. There's nothing we can do for her now.'

'Oh dear,' sobbed Kelly-Anne. 'We've never had anything like this happen at the Now to Zen. What a terrible accident.'

Corrie put an arm around her and led her away. 'I think you should call the manager so he can arrange to cut off the power, and then he'll probably want to call the police and the fire service to come and check it out.'

'Yes . . . of course. I'll get Mr Hawkins.' She hurried away, snivelling.

'Poor little thing,' said Corrie. 'She's had a shock.'

'She very nearly had a fatal one,' said Jack. He peered at the corpse, curious. 'I wonder why she got in the water with all her clothes on. And what's that gun doing in there? She hasn't been shot — there isn't any blood.' His sharp detective's eyes had spotted the small handgun, out of plain sight, beneath one of the flickering lights. He would have liked to fish it out and examine it, but that wasn't possible.

Corrie sensed his curiosity. 'Jack, this is not your problem. Let the local police deal with it. We'll just tell them we found the body and that will be an end of it. It's up to them to decide if it's suspicious, not you.'

'Right, and you put me down as an electrician. That was smart, wasn't it?'

Corrie pulled a face. 'How was I to know someone would be electrocuted?'

Both Richard and Penny Hawkins appeared, anxious and still wearing dressing gowns, so they had obviously retired for the night.

'Mr and Mrs Dawes?' He extended a hand. 'Dick Hawkins. I believe you and Kelly-Anne found the body? I've had maintenance turn off the power to the whirlpools and called the necessary authorities.'

'This is a terrible start to what was intended to be your relaxing break with us,' apologized Penny. 'Thank goodness you're an electrician, Mr Dawes, and recognized the danger.'

'Er . . . yes. Thank goodness.'

'Well, if you don't need us anymore, we'll go back to our room and get some sleep,' said Corrie. She hurried Jack away, before he started making any policeman-like observations concerning a submerged handgun. That was for somebody else to find.

CHAPTER FIVE

Tim Bennett never did get to enjoy Brightsea's vibrant night-life. At ten thirty, he had no sooner left the Now to Zen to discover the enticements of the brightly lit promenade, when a black limousine with tinted windows began to crawl along the kerb beside him. Eventually, it pulled up a few yards ahead. Two heavies in suits and dark glasses climbed out and blocked his path. He tried to sidestep them, but they grabbed his arms.

'Get in the car, Eddie.'

'Here, what's your game?' Tim tried to break free. 'My name isn't Eddie, it's Tim. You've got the wrong bloke. Now, bugger off and leave me alone.'

'We know who you are, Clayton. You just came out of that posh hotel. You can afford it with all the cash you nicked. Your wife tipped us off that's where you'd be, and the boss wants his money back.' They bundled him into the back of the car with one thug either side of him, like a menacing sandwich. The driver didn't speak or turn around, just put his foot down.

Tim was starting to get worried as well as angry. 'My wife? What's Miriam got to do with anything?'

One of them laughed. 'Is that what Della's calling herself these days?'

'Della? I don't know anyone called Della. And I haven't stolen any money. Stop the car and let me out.'

'You must be joking, mate. We've been looking for you for a long time. There's no way you're going anywhere until the boss has had a nice cosy chat.' He began cracking his knuckles.

'Look, this is all a mistake.' Tim was really scared now. He couldn't believe this was happening. It was like a terrifying nightmare, except he wasn't asleep. These blokes, whoever they were, meant business. 'Just take me back to the hotel and they'll confirm who I am.'

'Is that where you've hidden the money? We know you didn't leave it at your gaff. Della gave us that address, too. We took the place apart. Even pulled up the floorboards. Where'd you put it, Eddie? I'm guessing you didn't stash it away in a building society for the interest.' They laughed.

'I keep telling you, I haven't got your money and I don't know where it is.'

The big ugly one cracked his knuckles again. 'You will tell us, Eddie. Eventually.'

The car pulled up outside a padlocked warehouse on the outskirts of Brightsea. They manhandled Tim from the car and dragged him inside, his legs dangling. By now, he was so scared, he doubted his legs would have supported him anyway. Once inside, they turned on the bright lights that illuminated the deserted building. Then they tied him to a chair, in the middle of the vast storeroom, once used to house engineering equipment. Tim recognized crates bearing firearms labels and bricks of cocaine in brown wrappers. There were various tools lying on a pallet. One of the men picked up a pair of bolt cutters.

His mate stopped him. 'Wait until the boss gets here.' He grinned at Tim. 'He likes to watch this kind of thing. You'd be surprised how fast you'll get your memory back.'

Tim was terrified. 'You don't understand. My name's Timothy Bennett. I'm a used-car salesman. I don't know anything about any cash, I swear.'

'No. You won't swear — you'll scream. They all do. I've phoned the boss. He'll be here in half an hour. You got any booze?'

His partner produced a bottle of whisky and they sat down to wait.

* * *

It was gone midnight when the boss turned up. By this time, Tim was shaking and he had a suspicion that he'd wet himself or worse. If he knew where their bloody money was, he'd have told them, pretty damn fast. Now they were going to torture him for information he didn't have. He'd read about this kind of thing, heard reports on the news and seen films. Never, for a second, did he — a used-car salesman — think he'd actually get mixed up in it.

Headlights swept across the grimy windows, and moments later, the boss swaggered in, accompanied by four hefty bodyguards. He took one look at Tim and hit the roof.

'Who's this clown?' He turned on Tim's minders. 'That isn't Eddie Clayton, you bloody idiots!'

'I kept telling them,' Tim sobbed. 'They wouldn't believe me.'

The minders were scared now. The boss didn't tolerate cock-ups. 'He fitted the description, boss,' stammered one.

'That's right,' agreed the other. 'Six-foot-two, slim build with a beard and a tash. And he came out of that poncy spa place, where Della said he'd be. How were we to know?' There was a hint of desperation in his voice.

'Can I go now, please?' begged Tim. 'After all, it isn't me you want.' He laughed nervously. 'It was just a case of mistaken identity. No harm done. I won't say anything, I promise.'

'Sorry, chum,' said the boss. 'It doesn't work like that. Thanks to these two goons, you've seen everything now.

There's no way I can let you go.' He motioned to the goons in question. 'You know what to do.'

They untied Tim and were about to strong-arm him towards the door when it was kicked open and half a dozen thugs burst in. They were armed with various weapons designed to maim, dismember or exterminate. The rival gang leaders exchanged a few pertinent questions concerning the whereabouts of the missing money.

'OK, where's the cash, you cheating bastard?'

'You've got it, you double-crossing arsehole!'

'If I had it, I wouldn't be wasting my time talking to an ugly, shit-faced son of a bitch like you.'

'Hand it over and maybe I won't break your legs with this hammer.'

'OK, boys, let's get 'em.'

The two rival gangs began to lay into each other. Tim took advantage of the situation and ran for the door. He was beaten to it by the boss, who'd decided that discretion was the better part of valour and left the two gangs to fight it out. As he reached the exit, he flicked off the light and plunged the yelling, screaming melee into darkness and confusion. Once outside, he jumped into his Bentley and the driver spun the wheels, kicking up gravel, and sped away.

Tim ran as if his life depended on it. With hindsight, he decided it probably had. He only stopped, breathless, when he reached the beach. What if they came after him? He needed to hide until he was sure they weren't following. He ran over the pebbles, down the sand and hid behind one of the pillars under the pier. Exhausted with the effort and total terror, he fell into a disturbed sleep.

* * *

Detective Constable Jeff 'Noz' Nosworthy of the county constabulary had been at home and asleep when he got the call. Uniform had attended the scene of a sudden death at the Now to Zen Hotel and Spa and considered it suspicious enough to involve CID. Accordingly, DC Nosworthy reckoned at that time of the morning, and on a Sunday, it merited the attention of an officer higher up the pay scale, so he called DS Larry Bristow.

'What is it, Noz? Couldn't it wait until morning?'

'Apparently not, Sarge. They've found a body up at the hotel and spa.'

Bristow yawned. 'That place is full of bodies — most of 'em with more money than sense.'

'Yeah, but this one's dead. Electrocuted in a whirlpool, apparently.'

'Surely that's for the health-and-safety boys to sort out.'

'That's what I said, but the manager claims the spa's health and safety has only just been inspected and was found to be compliant. He reckons somebody must have tampered with the wires.'

DS Bristow sighed. 'OK, Noz, I'll meet you there. Has anyone contacted the boss? I think she'd want to be informed.'

* * *

Detective Inspector Lorraine Long was aptly named. She stood six-foot-three in her stockinged feet and had a reputation for getting the truth out of suspects, however long it took. Despite the unsocial hour, she was immaculately turned out in a dark blue trouser suit and white blouse. Her hair was scraped back in a bun, making her look even more intimidating than she actually was, and that wasn't easy. A uniformed constable lifted the police tape surrounding the whirlpool and she ducked under.

DS Bristow and DC Nosworthy were waiting for her at the poolside. Bristow was scruffy, by anybody's standards. Plain clothes for him meant faded jeans that had seen better days, with the baggy seat drooping precariously around his behind, and a greasy leather jacket. Grubby trainers completed the look. He maintained that his relaxed style enabled him to blend in with the villains, giving him the advantage of surprise. DC Nosworthy was wearing a suit and tie and well-polished shoes. He wouldn't have been comfortable doing his job in anything else.

First off, DI Long scrutinized the surroundings, taking in the entrance and exit and the ease of concealment between the pods. 'What have we got, Larry?'

'A dead woman, boss. The bloke who found her—' Bristow consulted his notes — 'was Rupert Dawes, an electrician. He confirmed, straight away, that she'd been electrocuted. The manager, Richard Hawkins, says that couldn't have been possible unless someone had interfered with the circuit.'

'Do we have an ID?'

'Not yet. I thought you would want to question the staff and the other guests. The manager has set aside a room we can use.'

DI Long peered at the body for some minutes. 'I want a full SOCO team down here and the pathologist, Doctor Nielsen. Nobody touches anything until I can be sure the electrics are safe. Maybe this Rupert Dawes knows what he's talking about. On the other hand, as he's an electrician, I can't be sure he isn't involved in what might turn out to be a murder.' She bent down and looked more closely. 'When SOCOs fish out that gun, I need a full check on it. And pull in this Dawes bloke — I'll question him when I'm ready.'

* * *

After breakfast, Corrie went off for a hot stone massage to melt away all the knots, aches and worries caused by finding a dead body. It was exactly what she'd brought Jack away to avoid and she'd seen the gleam of interest in his eyes. Even as the warm stones were being placed along her spine, she thought, grimly, that murders seemed to follow him around.

Jack took advantage of her absence to ring Bugsy on his mobile, at home. The phone rang twice then a familiar voice answered. It being Sunday morning, Bugsy was still chewing the last of his full English.

'Hello, guv. Are you having a relaxing time?' Bugsy sounded pleased to hear from him and Jack was similarly happy to be back in contact. Already, he was really missing the job and he'd only been gone a short time.

'Not really. Last night, Corrie and I found a dead body in a fancy whirlpool. The corpse was fully dressed and there was a gun beside her, but she hadn't been shot. She'd been electrocuted.'

'Blimey, guv, you certainly find 'em, don't you? I take it you handed it over to the local lads. Do they know who it is?'

'Not yet, they're still working on it. But it's the gun I'm interested in. I only got a brief look at it because Corrie pulled me away, but I'm pretty sure it was a Taurus Model 856. They're banned outright in the UK so it must have been smuggled in, probably from the US. It's a small-frame, short-barrelled revolver, easily concealed and intended for personal protection.'

'You seem to know a lot about it, guv.'

'That's because I saw one, recently, on the CCTV footage of a County Lines drugs operation, working out of London and into Kings Richington. It was never recovered, and we never caught the bloke who fired it, so there's an outside chance it could be the same one that's turned up here. Can you get Clive to isolate a picture of the gun from the CCTV then email it to my personal phone? I've left my police-issue one at home.'

'Yeah, course, but should you be getting involved, Jack? You know what the old man thinks about working on some-one else's patch, never mind what Mrs Dawes will say if she finds out.'

'The old man' was Chief Superintendent George Garwood, who headed up the Metropolitan Murder Investigation Team and was budget vigilant. He would definitely not condone one of his officers working for free on another DCS's territory, and without permission.

'I'm not intending to get involved. I just thought if I had a piece of intelligence that might help the local CID locate the killer — and I'm pretty sure this is a murder — it might speed up the investigation. That's all. You need to keep this under your hat, Bugsy. If I'm right, this is more than just a random killing.'

'OK, guv, I'll get Clive onto it, first thing tomorrow. I'll get back to you on your phone as soon as I've got anything. You can tell me if it's not a good time and you can't speak.'

This was more like it! Jack felt happier already.

CHAPTER SIX

Tim woke up under the pier, stiff and cold. His mouth felt gritty, and he guessed there was sand in it. For a few moments, he couldn't remember why he was there. He couldn't remember going on a bender and passing out. Then, suddenly, the events of the previous night returned with terrifying clarity. He jumped up and looked about him, as if he expected to see the thugs running down the beach to get him. Then he relaxed. It was early and there was just an old lady walking her dog.

He felt in the pocket of his jacket, which, incredibly, he was still wearing. Even more surprising was the discovery that he still had his wallet. He remembered he had intended to spend some cash in the nightspots of Brightsea. The money was still in there, along with his credit cards and driver's licence. He couldn't remember who the thugs thought he was, but if he hadn't been so bloody petrified, he might have had the presence of mind to prove to them he was Timothy Bennett. On the other hand, they hadn't been in the mood to listen to explanations, so they probably wouldn't have believed him. In their line of business, forgeries were commonplace.

He staggered up the beach and onto the promenade. Luckily, a taxi was returning from an early-morning fare and he hailed it. If the driver was curious about his dishevelled appearance, he said nothing and simply drove him along the coast to his home. Tim was so relieved to be safe, he gave him a large tip, something he never did. He thought, briefly, how surprised Mim would have been.

Mim! Dear God! She was still in the hotel — and presumably, so was the gangster that they'd thought was him. These men were dangerous. He had to get her out. He poured himself a large Scotch, and with alcohol came clarity. He had left his mobile behind in the hotel room, on the bedside table. His thinking at the time was that he didn't want Mim ringing him when he was having fun. Fun? Huh! He rang the number and mercifully, after a few rings, Miriam answered.

'Mim, it's me.' He heard her disgusted snort at the other end. 'No, listen. It's not what you think. I was kidnapped by a gang of thugs soon after I left the hotel. They took me to some sort of warehouse and they were going to cut off my fingers if I didn't tell them where the money was. Then, when the boss arrived, he saw it wasn't me they wanted and told them to kill me, because I'd seen them. It was sheer luck that I managed to get away. Another gang turned up and there was a fight. I escaped while they were knocking lumps off one another. Honestly, Mim, it was terrifying. One of the gangsters who looks like me is still in the hotel. He's dangerous. You need to get out of there and come home, fast.'

There was a heavy silence.

'Timothy Bennett, if that's the best excuse you can come up with, then don't bother. You're pathetic. You only want me home to cook your food and do your washing. And in any case, I couldn't leave here, even if I wanted to. They found a murdered woman after you left and the police have told us we have to stay until they've sorted it out. Go back to your barmaid and leave me to enjoy myself.' She ended the call.

Tim poured himself another whisky. So, the bloke who looked like him had killed somebody. From what the gang had said, Tim had a pretty good idea who the dead woman was. It was this Della person, who'd shopped her husband. Maybe he should tell the police.

No, they wouldn't believe him, either. There was nothing he could do. He finished the bottle of Scotch and eventually passed out on the bed.

* * *

Despite Dick and Penny's attempts to contain it, news of the dead body had spread like nits in a nursery. Staff and guests alike were discussing it. Kelly-Anne had assumed the celebrity status she craved, and regaled anyone who'd listen with lurid accounts of the body, with its staring eyes and twisted face. It was obvious she hadn't seen the gun or it would have added a juicy titbit to her witness account.

DI Long found herself parlously short of leads. Identification had proved virtually impossible. Nobody admitted to having seen the woman before, and although she was wearing a black tunic and trousers, she was definitely not a member of the Now to Zen staff. After the body had been taken away to Doctor Nielsen for a post-mortem, the DI's colleagues had shown a photograph of the victim's clothes to Penny Hawkins.

'No, that's definitely not a Now to Zen uniform. You can tell it's made of cheap material, the sort you'd find in a downmarket clothing store, and there's no logo on the tunic. She certainly didn't get it from us.'

'So why do you think she was masquerading as a member of staff?' asked DS Bristow.

'I've no idea. She'd have been found out very soon if she'd tried to treat somebody. All our practitioners are dedicated professionals. She'd have been unmasked in an instant. What concerns me is how she managed to get in. Staff all wear lanyards with their names and a photo ID. Security is very tight. As you will have observed, we have professionally trained doormen minding all the entrances and exits. The public can't just wander in and out as they please. The Now to Zen is a haven of peace and solitude, a retreat where guests can be assured of privacy and seclusion, especially as they spend much of the time half-naked, having treatments.'

The pathology report, although prompt, was not helpful. It confirmed that the woman had, indeed, been electrocuted. The current had quite simply stopped her heart, wet skin having a hundred times less resistance than when dry. Estimated time of death was around eleven thirty, roughly an hour before she was found. Her age was thought to be anything between forty and fifty, and she had, at some time in the past, had a baby. There was no match on the police database for her fingerprints or DNA.

Strangely, the report noted that the distal phalange of each little finger had been crudely amputated, long enough ago for them to be healed. She had undergone cheap, foreign dental work, so no help with dental records, and her hair was home-bleached. The tox report recorded that she had consumed a good deal of gin prior to her death, and she had a cocaine habit, to the extent that she had a perforated septum. No birthmarks or tattoos.

Certainly not the kind of person you'd expect to find in a classy place like the Now to Zen, surmised Lorraine Long. *What the hell was she doing there?*

The gun didn't reveal anything useful. It had been wiped clean of fingerprints before it went in the water and it wasn't a type familiar to DI Long and her team. It had been sent to Ballistics to see if they could add anything useful, but if Lorraine had been a betting woman, she would have put money on it not having been fired recently. The crucial information came from the SOCO engineer. There was clear evidence that the wiring of the whirlpool lights had been purposely tampered with, to make the water lethal. It was definitely murder and not an accident. But it still didn't explain what the 'lady in black' was doing in there. And why had she brought a gun with her? That was assuming it *belonged* to her. Had she known her life was in danger? Was the gun for personal protection?

If it was, it hadn't worked.

* * *

Lorraine was pacing up and down in the meditative relaxation lounge that they'd been allocated as a makeshift incident room. She was brainstorming with Larry and Noz.

'Doctor Nielsen puts time of death at around eleven thirty on Saturday night. The body was discovered by a member of staff and two punters, Mr and Mrs Dawes, half an hour later, when they went for their midnight dip.'

'That's interesting,' said Larry, reading his notes, 'because the doormen are adamant that nobody entered or left the premises after ten thirty. All earlier comings and goings had been identified and logged. Last person to come in was Louis, the sports coach, at ten. It was his day off and he'd been out having what he described as a "cocktail workout" with a girlfriend, in her flat. I get the impression he's something of a player, but no form and no indication that he's a murderer. Last person to leave was a guest, Mr Timothy Bennett, a used-car salesman. He stormed out around ten thirty, after a row with his wife during dinner, and so far, he hasn't checked back in. His wife, Miriam, is still here and doesn't seem in the least concerned. When questioned, she said, "He'll be lying, blind drunk, in some tart's bed." Regardless of what we might think of his behaviour, I guess that gives him a pretty tight alibi.'

'Our victim could have broken in earlier and hidden somewhere,' suggested Noz.

'So how come there's no sign of a break-in?' Larry asked. 'And security say definitely not. They're confident she would have been spotted at some time during their patrols. They're a reliable team, hired by the Now to Zen from an independent security firm, at an eye-watering monthly fee.'

'Unless she hid in someone's room,' mused Noz. 'They wouldn't have patrolled people's rooms.'

Lorraine frowned in concentration. 'So what we're saying is, unless the murderer sneaked in somehow, killed our victim, then sneaked back out again — which security claim is impossible . . .'

'It means that he or she is still here — either a guest or a member of staff,' concluded Noz. 'It could have been the murderer's room she'd been hiding in.'

'Any thoughts on our next move, boss?' asked Larry.

'Why don't we fingerprint everyone, see if anybody has form?' suggested Noz brightly.

Lorraine sighed. 'DC Nosworthy, we can't go around demanding fingerprints from people without their consent, unless we have good reason to suspect them of having committed an offence, and so far, we don't have anybody in the frame. Read your PACE.'

They were digesting this information when DI Long glanced through the lounge window and spotted Abbie and Antonio hurrying past, followed by several porters, wheeling their luggage on trolleys. They were heading towards a private Jefferson taxi, destined for the airport.

Lorraine was on her feet and her head shot out of the door, like a moray eel from its lair. The similarity to a moray eel didn't end there. She could be vicious when challenged and was capable of seizing her prey and inflicting serious damage, if only verbally.

'Excuse me. Where do you think you're going?'

'Monaco,' replied Antonio and carried on walking.

'Didn't you get the police notice that nobody is allowed to leave until they're released by me?'

'Yeah, but that doesn't apply to us,' said Abbie. 'My father is Carter Jefferson III. He owns this hotel and a whole bunch of others, all over the world.'

DI Long was not to be thwarted by name-dropping. 'I don't care if your father is president of the United States, Indiana Jones and Batman, all rolled into one. This hotel is the scene of a murder and nobody leaves until I say so.'

'You can't do that!' yelled Antonio, furious.

'I think you'll find I can. Now, go back to your room, until I've had time to question you.'

'We don't have a room, we have a private spa suite,' said Abbie, haughtily. Then to Antonio, 'Come along, honey, I'll get Daddy's lawyers onto this. It stinks.'

Larry watched them trail back inside. 'That told her, boss. They think they're above the law, if they've got money.'

'All the same, I doubt I'll be able to hold them once the lawyers get stuck in, so we need to find who killed our "lady in black" — and fast.'

* * *

Most treatments had been temporarily postponed. The hotel was crawling with uniformed coppers, preventing anyone from entering or leaving, and taking names, addresses and time-consuming statements, which would prove largely pointless. They had closed off the whirlpool room entirely — not that there was much enthusiasm to use it, after what had happened. Dick and Penny decided there was little point starting courses of meditation and therapy, only to have to stop in mid-experience, because either the practitioner or the guest was called to account for their whereabouts at the time of the murder. The guests were assured that they would be compensated financially as a result.

'This is going to cost the company a fortune,' observed Dick. 'The accounts already indicate that this branch of the Now to Zen is haemorrhaging money. We'll have Jefferson's auditors down on us, if we don't improve soon.'

'Why should we worry?' said Penny. 'The corporation is absolutely loaded — it's obscene. It's hardly our fault if some woman managed to sneak in off the streets and get herself murdered.'

'Do you think that's what happened?'

Penny looked surprised. 'What else could it be?'

CHAPTER SEVEN

Complimentary afternoon tea was being served in the Caribbean Lounge. Guests sat around eating cupcakes and nibbling little triangular sandwiches, under authentic-looking palm trees. The parrots, perched among the fronds, were less realistic, as Rita discovered when she tried to feed one a biscuit. The atmosphere was somewhat strained.

Sir Marcus motioned to a waiter, who shimmered effortlessly to his side. 'If this is the Caribbean Lounge, is there any chance of a tot of rum with my tea, d'you think?'

'Certainly, sir.' The waiter went to fetch it.

'Are you a navy man, Sir Marcus?' asked Corrie. She had noticed his beard and moustache, but was asking more to make conversation than anything. '"Splicing the main brace", and all that.'

'Not any longer, Corrie. I'm in the import–export business, now.'

'That's interesting,' she replied politely, even though it wasn't. 'What sort of goods do you import and export?'

Before he could answer, the door burst open and Louis jogged in, muscles rippling beneath a spotless white vest and shorts, curly hair bouncing in a sporty, textured crop, and a cheery smile showing dazzling white teeth.

'OK, ladies, enough of this slacking. We're going to start beasting it up. Everybody outside on the lawn for my "Stay Young and Beautiful" class. Ace reps for hams, gluts, pecs, abs — you name it.'

'I would, if I knew what language that was,' muttered Miriam. Without make-up, it was obvious that the thirty-nine she admitted to wasn't within hailing distance of the truth. Tim hadn't come back, so she'd assumed he didn't intend to spend any more time at the spa with her. That story he'd spun her was ludicrous — the ramblings of a man who'd spent too much time watching gangster films on TV. She realized she didn't much care who he was with. The poor, misguided soul was welcome to him.

They trooped outside, where a stiff breeze from the Urals was causing the seagulls to fly backwards. Louis was undeterred. 'Right, marching on the spot, to warm up. Anything I should know about? Bad backs, floating kneecaps, weak bladders? Ha ha ha! No, I'm sorry, love, you're absolutely right, a weak bladder isn't funny. I was just trying to lighten the mood. If you need to — you know — be excused, just . . . er . . .' He was about to say 'piss off', but realized, just in time, that wasn't funny, either. 'You just slip away, my love. Is everybody warm now?'

Rita was marching out of time with everybody else. Louis called out to her. 'March on both feet, Rita, love. Did you bring any trainers? Only slingbacks aren't best suited for this type of exercise.' She'd been in two minds about 'warming up'. The last time she'd been properly warm was in 1980, when she got stuck in a lift with the front row of the Clitheroe rugby team.

Corrie joined in, more for something to do besides eat cake. She hadn't seen Jack since breakfast. The last she'd heard, he'd been summoned by the CID's senior investigating officer, DI Lorraine Long, for questioning. She guessed it would be her turn next. She hoped he'd managed to resist the temptation to offer 'advice'.

Louis ploughed cheerfully on, despite a less-than-enthusiastic class. 'Now, what I want you to do next, ladies, is gently squat down, then spring back up and lunge forward onto the right foot. Your own right foot for preference, Rita, love. This is to sculpt your gluteus maximus into a nice shape. What? It's your butt, dear. Your bum cheeks. Watch Dorothy, everyone. That's the way to do it. Obviously, horse riding is the perfect exercise for strengthening your *derrière*. I bet you have a pelvic floor like a trampoline.' He winked at her.

Corrie wasn't a copper's wife for nothing. While she was bobbing up and down and lunging, she was surreptitiously considering the folk at the spa, and trying to work out who might have either colluded in — or committed — the murder of the unfortunate woman they'd found in the whirlpool. She realized she was spoiled for choice.

Her train of thought was interrupted by Louis bellowing, 'Right, lovely ladies. Now we're going to do some jazzerobics.' He turned up the pumping music. 'What I want you to do here is move those funky bodies to the boogie beat. Let's go, girls!'

Corrie decided her body was more chunky than funky, but carried on anyway. Upwind of her, Rita let out a ferocious fart every time she bent down. On her left, Dorothy leaned across and asked, furtively, 'Do you think he's wearing a thingy . . . you know . . . a support whatsit under those shorts? Or is that bulge all him, do you suppose?'

Corrie smiled and shook her head. Returning to her deliberations, she knew that if Jack was SIO, he'd be looking at the MMO — motive, means and opportunity.

The means had been fairly well established. She imagined that anyone who understood electricity and wiring would have been able to find a way to connect the water in the pool to the mains. Opportunity wouldn't have been a problem. Guests were free to use the twilight whirlpool room whenever they liked. As far as she was aware, nobody questioned or monitored the visits. That left motive. That was the tricky one. In order to establish motive, you needed to know something about the victim's lifestyle and her contacts, before you could work out who might want her dead. Nobody knew who this woman was. Unless, of course, it was simply a random killing. She discounted that. Random killings didn't happen in massively expensive Now to Zen hotels — did they?

'Come along, now, Corrie.' Louis's voice cut short her reflections. 'You're not putting your thighs into it. We want to tone up those wobblers, don't we?'

* * *

After a long wait, Jack was finally admitted to the meditative relaxation lounge — now a makeshift incident room. It smelled of lavender and chamomile. DI Long was sitting on one side of a treatment table, adapted to serve as a desk. She motioned to him to sit down opposite. The sound of falling water from an infinity pool was designed to relax and refresh the occupants, helping them to forget about anything that had been playing on their minds. DI Long had just the opposite intention. She looked down at her screen, to refresh her memory.

'You're Rupert Dawes, the man who found the body.' She made it sound more like an accusation than a question.

DS Bristow was sitting beside her, looking serious and making notes. DC Nosworthy stood by the door, watchful, as if he was expecting Jack to make a sudden dash for freedom.

Jack smiled pleasantly. 'That's right, but please, just call me Jack.'

She didn't smile back. 'Why? You're registered under the name of Rupert.'

'Yes, I know. Jack's just a nickname. You know — jackdaws, like the birds? Nicknames are quite common in the pol— . . . er . . . among electricians.'

'What were you doing in the whirlpool room at midnight?'

'My wife, Corrie, and I had finished dinner and our spa buddy, Kelly-Anne, had come to take us to finish off the evening, relaxing in a whirlpool pod, but when we got there, there was a body in—'

'And being an electrician, you realized straight away that the woman had been electrocuted.'

'Er . . . something like that, but—'

'Did you know the deceased, Mr Dawes?'

'No. Corrie and I only arrived that morning. We didn't know anybody here. We live in Kings Richington.'

'Where were you at eleven thirty that evening?' demanded Bristow.

Jack was immediately interested. 'Is that the estimated time of death?'

'Never mind,' barked DI Long. 'Just answer the question.'

'Well, like I just told you, I was having dinner with my wife. She had filet mignon and I had corned beef hash. We were laughing because—'

'Did you leave the dining room at any time?'

'No, not until Kelly-Anne came for us.'

'Not even to go to the lavatory?' DI Long eyeballed him in a manner he found most disturbing.

'Well, I may have just popped out for a—'

'Did you or didn't you?' growled Bristow.

'Yes, I believe I did.'

'Were you gone long enough to "pop" down to the whirlpool room, Mr Dawes?'

'No. Why would I do that?' Jack was beginning to real-ize that this was a pincer interrogation, like he and Bugsy had employed many times with suspects. But surely, they didn't think he was a suspect?

DI Long, being the senior half of the tag team, was the more aggressive and the more imaginative of the two. 'Let me tell you what I believe happened. You slipped out during dinner and went down to the whirlpools, where you'd planned to meet your troublesome mistress. You got there first, and using your electrical skills, you fixed the lights, probably frayed the wires, so that the current was diverted directly into the water. Then you smuggled her in when the doorman wasn't looking and took her down to the unoccupied pool room, where you quarrelled. She wouldn't agree to leave you alone, so you pushed her in, knowing she would be instantly killed. Then you went back to the dining room and calmly finished your meal, planning to act surprised when you later discovered the body, with your wife and the spa employee, Kelly-Anne Something, as witnesses. How am I doing so far?'

Jack was stunned. He couldn't believe a police officer, even one as ruthless as DI Long, could construct such a wild and totally inaccurate series of events. 'That's absolute nonsense! She wasn't my mistress — I'd never seen the woman before in my life. What would be my motive for killing a perfect stranger?'

Bristow joined the attack. 'I put it to you that she wasn't a stranger, she was your bit on the side, and she was threatening to tell your wife what you'd been up to. We checked out Mrs Dawes. She's a very successful caterer with three lucrative businesses. Coriander's Cuisine is doing very well, financially. On the other hand, we couldn't trace any electricians called Rupert Dawes. You couldn't afford for your wife to kick you out, could you?'

Jack realized this was getting serious and he'd have to come clean. 'Look, I'm not an electrician — I'm a police officer.' He reached inside his jacket for his warrant card, then realized he didn't have it. Corrie had made him leave it at home as a subliminal gesture to prove his genuine commitment to leaving the job behind. 'I'm Detective Inspector Jack Dawes of the Metropolitan Murder Investigation Team.'

'Of course you are,' scoffed Bristow. 'And I'm the chief constable's Aunt Fanny.'

Jack couldn't believe this was happening. 'You can check it out if you don't believe me.'

'We don't know what to believe,' said DI Long. 'First you call yourself Rupert, then you change it to Jack. You say you never left the dining room, then you say you did.'

'But the best part is that five minutes ago, you were an electrician, but now you're really a copper. You must think we came down the Ouse on a pedalo.' Bristow laughed. 'What d'you reckon, boss? Shall I caution and arrest him on suspicion of murder?'

'Not yet.' She stood up, slowly unravelling until all six-foot-three towered over Jack, then she scowled down at him. 'You're free to go for now, Dawes, but nobody leaves the hotel. We'll want to question you again. Hand over your phone.'

'What?'

'You heard. Give me your phone. You can have it back after we've checked your calls — that's if we don't find anything suspicious.'

This will put an end to it, thought Jack. Surely they had to believe he was a copper when he showed them a police-issue mobile? Then he remembered that he'd left that at home, too. He only had his personal phone. Speechless, he pulled it from his pocket and handed it over. She nodded to DC Nosworthy to open the door and let Jack out.

After he'd gone, Larry said, 'I don't think he did it, do you, boss?'

'No. He was like a rabbit in headlights. And we certainly don't have enough evidence to arrest him. It's all circumstantial at best. Mind you, I'd have been more suspicious if he'd mentioned the gun in his witness statement. He obviously knows nothing about that.'

Bristow nodded. 'I think we rattled him enough to be sure he'll decide to tell us, if he's keeping anything back. D'you reckon he's a detective from the Met, like he claims?'

She laughed. 'Nah. Course not. He's not smart enough to be a woodentop, let alone a detective inspector.'

* * *

It was early evening before Jack was free to go and look for Corrie. He found her in one of the treatment rooms, lying on a couch. Whale music and the whooshing sounds of the ocean were playing in the background and the lighting was subdued. He hardly recognized her in the gloom.

'What's that stuff on your face?'

'It's a whelk and wheatgerm face mask,' mumbled Corrie. 'It's to restore my skin's natural radiance and I'm not supposed to talk. It's starting to harden.'

He peered closer. 'It looks like mouldy shredded wheat.'

'Never mind that. Where have you been all day?'

'Being put through the mincer by a lady detective inspector. Honestly, Corrie, I never realized what a terrifying experience it is, being accused of a crime and sounding guilty under interrogation, when you know very well that you're innocent.'

'Wha—?' Corrie's eyes widened with shock, although the rest of her face remained immobile.

'They said they believed the dead woman was my mistress and that I killed her to stop her from telling you. They checked the financial status of your businesses and decided that I was a kept man and I couldn't afford for you to throw me out.'

The idea was so ludicrous, Corrie wanted to laugh, but with a stiff face, it came out as a series of throaty burps.

'Thanks to you putting me down as an impoverished electrician, they reckoned I had means, motive and opportunity. It was game, set and match. In the end, I had to tell them I'm a copper, but I could see they didn't believe me and had no intention of checking it out. I planned to ring Garwood and get him to vouch for me, but she confiscated my phone.' It was then that Jack remembered asking Bugsy to email him a picture of the Taurus 856. Bloody hell! If they saw that, he was really in trouble. He didn't doubt that DI Long would consider it evidence enough to arrest him on suspicion of involvement in a murder. After all, a similar weapon had been found at the scene. 'Corrie, can I borrow your phone? It's urgent!'

She shook her head, then hissed through congealing lips. 'Left it at home.' Carlene had persuaded Corrie not to take her phone. She'd argued that, knowing Mrs D, she wouldn't be able to help herself from ringing in every five minutes, to see how the Cuisine was holding up without her. Carlene had said she needed to chill out, totally. Incommunicado — cold turkey — was the only way.

Damn! Now he'd have to find a landline. He needed to speak to Bugsy and tell him on no account was he to email the photo of the gun.

He headed for reception. It was mayhem. The queue of people wanting to check out stretched across the lobby and into the lounge. The atmosphere was febrile with furious guests, incensed because they were being told they had to stay until DI Long was satisfied with their statements and released them.

'You can't keep me here, I have important business in Japan,' said one angry gentleman, his luggage already on a trolley.

'Why are we being treated as if we've committed a crime?' a similarly outraged lady wanted to know.

'I demand to speak to the officer in charge. I'm a personal friend of the chief constable. I'm here on medical advice.' This from a man whose stay at the spa, Jack deduced, had clearly not had the desired result. He was overweight, florid and stressed. The only pounds he appeared to have lost would have been from his bank account — and probably a good few grand of them, at that.

When Jack finally reached the reception desk and asked to use the phone, he was told DI Long had decreed there was to be no landline communications, in or out, until she gave permission. He returned to his room, contemplating his next step out of the ridiculous situation he had found himself in. But it was already too late.

CHAPTER EIGHT

Rainbow had been assigned to David as his personal spa attaché. Her pre-consultation background information was that he was seriously withdrawn, socially anxious and lacking in confidence. The online self-assessment form he had completed was ambiguous. It gave the impression that he disliked change, but nevertheless, he wanted to move on. He was plagued, he claimed, with self-doubt and an obsessive, destructive focus on his past. Her brief was to read his aura, and thus informed, she would guide him to better overall health and wellbeing.

For his part, David had been told by the Jefferson US IT manager to blend in with the other guests, behave like he was there to be treated and do whatever it took to identify the cyber thief. That way, he wouldn't arouse suspicion, and he could find the best way to access the digital accounts. Cyber thieves were sophisticated. They could breach security measures and intercept data, so it wouldn't be easy. He was to report back to headquarters as soon as he had anything.

Rainbow's auraology room had no tables or couches, just big cushions on the floor. She preferred quiet, natural light, so there were no candles or music to corrupt her ability to connect with her client's human energy field. She and

David sat cross-legged opposite each other. She stared at him, or sometimes through him, for a long time.

'Your aura is not a single entity. It's made up of seven different layers that intertwine to form a relatively cohesive body. These layers can be divided into two planes, the physical and the spiritual. It's my job to locate whatever it is that needs repairing.' She put the heel of her hand on David's forehead. 'Close your eyes.'

He did as he was told. As a software engineer, he was sceptical of all things mystical, believing that if he couldn't apply an algorithm to it, it didn't exist. In this case, however, it was a means to an end, so he carried on, despite his conviction that the whole charade was a waste of time.

She frowned, then increased the pressure. 'I don't understand. You say that you suffer from social anxiety, you dislike change and need help to connect with others. You mentioned destructive aspects of your past that you wish to leave behind.'

'Er . . . yes, that's right.' *My mother, mainly*, he thought. *Blimey, how very Freudian.* But there was nothing psychosexual about it. He just wished she'd stop interfering every time he tried to develop a relationship with a girl. Her interrogations and criticisms inevitably drove them away. At the present rate, he'd end up a crusty old bachelor, living a slow death with a couple of cats for company. That wasn't what he wanted at all.

Rainbow didn't buy it. 'What you say doesn't align with your aura at all. It's very definitely blue — the colour of a strong seeker of the truth, a concern for rule-keeping, law and insight. Also, your feminine side has an abundance of colour. That means you're focusing most of your attention on the future, not the past.'

David felt decidedly uncomfortable. He had submitted to this reading, believing it to be a load of hippy-dippy, esoteric gibberish, designed to extract as much money from the punter as possible, before they realized it was meaningless. Rainbow, either by coincidence or a genuine gift, was getting dangerously close to the real reason he was there. He decided he should end the session before she came any closer. 'Maybe this just isn't the right treatment for me.'

Rainbow shook her head. 'Virtually all healing comes through the astral plane. I'm never wrong.' She looked at the space above his head. 'There's a band of colour, stretching like an arc above you. This tells me what your hopes and goals are. It's bright red, which means you seek more rewards and better business prospects. I don't remember you mentioning that at the beginning of your reading. You want me to believe you are weak, inadequate and vulnerable. Your aura tells me you are nothing of the kind.' She stood up. 'I don't know why you're really here, David, but I know it isn't to take my help seriously.' She opened the door and stood back, indicating that he should leave. 'You won't be charged for this consultation.'

David went back to his room. That hadn't gone at all well and it seemed that he'd upset Rainbow, which he hadn't intended to do. He found her very attractive. Normally, he didn't bother to register what a girl looked like, having no real expectations of ever getting to know her while his mother was on his case. But more importantly, he needed to be more convincing if he was to get to the source of the fraud. Once his cover was blown, he'd be of no use to Jefferson's US IT company in finding the culprit. He or she would cover their tracks and disappear into cyberspace.

* * *

DS Bristow placed Jack's phone in a plastic evidence bag. He was on the way to hand it over to Digital Forensics for examination. It was unlocked, so it should be relatively easy for them to find anything incriminating. Suddenly, the screen lit up and it rang. The ringtone, which made him jump, was a police siren. Jack had chosen it so that he'd hear it when he was among the crowd at rugby matches. Bristow looked at it. There was no caller number displayed. This could well be one of Dawes's crooked associates. He considered that identifying the caller was more important than worrying about contaminating fingerprints, so he took it out of the bag between finger and thumb, swiped the green button and spoke just the one word. 'Hello?'

A male voice answered, 'Is that you, guv? It's me, Bugsy. Did you get the gun?'

'Who is this?' Bristow demanded. There was a pause, then the phone went dead. There was an email with an attachment. He opened it. It was a photograph of a handgun. If he wasn't much mistaken, it was the same type that they'd fished out of the pool. Bingo! Got the smug bastard! He hurried to show it to DI Long.

* * *

Back in the MIT office in Kings Richington, Bugsy frowned. Who the hell was that on the other end of Jack's phone? It certainly wasn't Jack.

'Was that the boss?' asked DC Williams.

'Is he having a restful holiday, Sarge? I mean, sir.' DC Fox remembered Bugsy was acting DI.

Bugsy rang worried fingers through his hair. He guessed it wouldn't hurt to let the team know as much as he did. 'No, to both those questions, and for Christ's sake, don't call me "sir" — it makes me nervous. A situation has arisen at the spa hotel. The guvnor and Mrs Dawes found a murdered woman. She'd been electrocuted in one of those posh whirlpools.'

'I went in one of those once. It was at the lido in Pontypridd,' recalled Aled. 'You have water swooshing all around you. It's like sitting naked in a car wash, only more expensive.'

'I thought Jack had taken a holiday to get away from murders,' observed Sergeant Parsloe. 'He might just as well have stayed here and waited for a local one. Damn sight cheaper.'

'True,' said Bugsy. 'But the thing is — there was a gun in the water alongside the corpse. The guv thought he recognized the type from the CCTV of a County Lines shooting and wanted a pic to confirm it. Clive isolated the frame and I emailed it to Jack's phone, but when I rang just now to make sure he'd got it, someone else answered.'

'Did you ask who it was?' said Aled.

Bugsy scowled. 'No, of course I didn't, you Celtic twerp! I'm hardly going to start a conversation about a gun I'm not supposed to know anything about and get Jack into trouble, am I?'

'No, I s'pose not.' Aled thought about it. 'Mind you, if that had happened on our patch — someone was murdered by electrocution — and the bloke who found the body had registered his occupation as an electrician . . .'

'. . . You'd be suspicious, at the very least,' finished Gemma.

'And you'd most likely confiscate his phone, to see what he'd been up to,' agreed Bugsy. 'Bloody hell! I bet the bloke answering Jack's phone was from CID. And now I've landed Jack right in it.'

'What do we do, Sarge?'

'I'm not sure we can do anything without making things a bloody sight worse. Even if we somehow confirm that the guv is a copper, not an electrician, that wouldn't necessarily prove he wasn't a dodgy one.'

Gemma frowned. 'Surely they don't seriously believe that the DI would kill anyone? That's crackers.'

'Listen,' said Bugsy, 'if you're a DI looking to make a name for yourself, and you suspect you've got a chance to nail another DI for what might turn out to be a murder connected to police corruption, you're going to go for it, aren't you?'

'But suspicion isn't evidence,' asserted Aled.

Bugsy was doubtful. 'No, son, it isn't. But it can seem like evidence, if you look at it hard enough.'

* * *

When DI Long had first seen the photo of the revolver on DI Dawes's phone, she'd thought all her birthdays and Christmases had come at once. Ballistics had come back to her with a report on the gun that was found in the whirlpool at the spa. It was, they said, a Taurus Model 856, manufactured in Brazil and smuggled into the UK, where it's illegal. No doubt it had been passed around various members of the criminal fraternity before turning up in Brightsea. No fingerprints, but there was one distinguishing mark — a very small but distinctive dent on the barrel. Probably from having been dropped or thrown at some time.

'But here's the really good news,' she said to DS Bristow. 'The photo of the gun on Dawes's phone has been examined by Digital Forensics. They enlarged it and they have identified the dent. Larry, it's the same gun.'

'So how come Dawes had a photo of it on his phone, if he isn't involved?' asked Bristow.

'And who is this Bugsy character?' wondered DI Long. 'Sounds like the nickname of a gangster, to me. And why did he ask if Dawes had "got the gun"?'

'Maybe Dawes was meant to recover it from the pool, but there were witnesses, so he couldn't. Can I arrest him now, boss?'

'Yes, Larry. We've got enough to pull him in for further questioning.' Lorraine was pleased with the way things were going. She didn't yet have enough to charge Dawes, but she was pretty certain he was a bent copper, taking a bung from organized crime gangs. There could be a promotion in it, if she managed to crack the whole operation. She liked the sound of Detective *Chief* Inspector Lorraine Long. 'Let's go and get him.'

CHAPTER NINE

Jack was in the foyer, waiting for the lift, when DS Bristow and DC Nosworthy quietly materialized either side of him and took hold of his arms. He realized it was too late to contact Bugsy and tell him not to send the image of the Taurus 856 to his phone. They already had it.

DI Long cautioned him, then arrested him on suspicion of having committed a number of offences connected to organized crime, including the murder of the, as yet, unidentified woman. She didn't have enough evidence to charge him with wounding a police officer during a drugs raid, but she could add that later, after he'd confessed. She certainly had enough to hold him until then.

'You're making a big mistake,' Jack heard himself say, as they cuffed him and led him away to the waiting police car. *Isn't that what all villains say when they're nicked?* he thought. Now he knew how they felt. Fortunately, most of the guests had given up trying to check out, so there wasn't too big an audience in the hotel reception area when they frogmarched Jack away.

Dick was horrified by the whole debacle. First a dead woman in the twilight pool, now a guest taken away in handcuffs, suspected of her murder. Money was inexplicably leaking from the digital accounts and Timothy Bennett had done a runner. Could it get any worse? Dick fully expected the Jefferson lawyers to move in any day now and close them down. They might just as well, because the police had prohibited him from accepting any new bookings until further notice.

The Buncombe sisters were fascinated. They didn't get this kind of excitement in Nether Babington. For Peggy, the only contretemps she'd ever had with the police had been about leaving a trail of muck on the road. Dorothy thought Jack Dawes was very handsome. She hoped he'd been arrested for something glamorous like spying or diamond smuggling and not just a parking fine. In the right light, and if you squinted a bit, he could easily pass for James Bond.

Sir Marcus was sitting in the guest lounge, tasting his first single malt of the day. *Poor sod*, he thought, as they led Jack past. *They've fitted him up for it.* Sir Marcus knew about the dead woman, electrocuted in the whirlpool. He'd been as surprised as everybody else. But he thought it very unlikely that the Dawes bloke was responsible. It was obvious the man knew nothing about electricity when he'd talked about coloured wires and fuse boxes. In fact, he was pretty sure he was a copper. He guessed it wouldn't deter that woman detective, though. She was doggedly determined to arrest somebody. 'Rottweiler' didn't even come close.

From the window of the private penthouse suite, Antonio spotted the police car draw up outside. He watched the cops bundle someone in the back and drive off, and he was sure, like Sir Marcus, that the man had been fitted up. But so what? If it meant they were all free to go, he didn't care who took the blame. Abbie was down in a luxury treatment room, having a diamond chakra massage, or some such mystical nonsense, so he didn't have to explain his obvious unease. He had to get out of this damn country. Where the hell were the lawyers?

Fred and Rita had just come back from what had been promoted as 'A Slow and Gentle Yoga Session for Seniors', with a dedicated yogini. Fred was bent double.

'I warned you not to try that one-legged pigeon,' Rita scolded. 'The last time you bent down to put your socks on, it took three osteopaths to straighten you out. You're too old for such antics.'

'Nonsense, Mother. I'm still a young man. When Mozart was my age, he'd been dead for thirty years.'

'What's that got to do with anything, you daft old barmpot? Mind you, I'm not a hundred per cent sure that girl knew what she was doing. Every time she leaned over me, I got a terrible whiff of gin and garlic sausage.' As they tottered past the foyer towards the lift, they spotted Jack on the way out with his escort.

'Well, I'll go to t'foot of our stairs!' Fred exclaimed. 'Mother, did you see that?'

'I did, Dad.'

'What do you reckon he's done?'

'Must be summat bad if it needed three plain-clothes bobbies to feel his collar. And as for that policewoman — did you see the face on her? I wouldn't give her any back answers, if I were him.'

Kelly-Anne thought that as a *boni fido* spa buddy, she should inform Mrs Dawes that Mr Dawes most probably wouldn't be back for dinner. She found Corrie, lurking by the kitchens, trying hard not to peek in to see what kind of equipment they had.

'Hello, Mrs Dawes. I'm Kelly-Anne, your spa buddy.'

'Yes, I know. You don't need to say that every time we meet.'

'Well, actually I do, because we're given these scripts with phrases that we're supposed to keep using. That's one of them. I'm also supposed to use "power words", like "awesome", "impressive" and "charming".'

'Go on then,' said Corrie, trying not to laugh.

'I've just seen three impressive police officers handcuff charming Mr Dawes and take him outside to an awesome police car.'

'What?' Corrie jumped back several feet with shock, narrowly missing a waiter backing out of the swing doors with a tray of food. 'When was this?'

'Just now.'

Corrie sprinted down the plush hallway and through the foyer to the outside door, just in time to see the police car speeding away. There were uniformed constables on either side of the entrance, to prevent people coming in or leaving.

'Where's that car going?' she asked one of them.

'To the police station, madam.' Then, more quietly, 'I understand DI Long has arrested the man who murdered the woman in the pool.'

'Oh no she bloody well hasn't!' Corrie assured him.

* * *

When they arrived at the police station, Jack asked for a phone call. He would ring Garwood and ask him to sort out this mess.

'As a serving police officer, I know that a detained person has the right to have their whereabouts notified, so I'd like you to inform my wife. Also, I'm allowed one telephone call. I'd like to make it now, please.'

DI Long looked scathing. 'You could have learned that from a crime drama on TV. If you really were a police officer, you would also know that both those requests can be delayed or denied by an inspector — that's me.'

Jack was exasperated. 'Well, do it yourself, then. Ring Detective Chief Superintendent George Garwood at Kings Richington Station. He's my boss. He'll vouch for me. While you're wasting time with me, the real killer could be getting away.' *Listen to yourself*, thought Jack. *That's something else villains always say.*

DI Long's brow furrowed. 'Sergeant Bristow, remind me. Where have I seen a report about Kings Richington?'

'It was during the operation to infiltrate encrypted communications, boss. Drug dealers were using dedicated phone lines to peddle drugs out of London and into Kings Richington and various other urban areas. There was a suspicion that certain police officers had been involved in County Lines for personal financial gain.'

DI Long pounced. 'So that's what you were up to, Dawes. We might be out in the sticks as far as you're concerned, but we know that large-scale, multi-faceted criminal operations are going on in London, where the real action takes place. It's run by career criminals and their associates. The cooperation of a large network of corrupt police officers is more than just a suspicion. So if you really are a copper, I believe you're a corrupt one.'

Bristow joined in with the verbal hectoring. 'Ballistics have confirmed that the gun we found next to the corpse, and the one pictured on your phone, is the exact same one that was used to wound a police officer in a drugs raid.'

Jack groaned in frustration. 'I know. That's what I've been trying to tell you. It was never recovered, and we never caught the criminal who fired it. I guessed that, as it was unusual, there was an outside chance it could be the same one that's turned up here. Smuggled guns get circulated around the underworld like dodgy passports. That's why I asked for the image from the CCTV to be sent to my phone, so that I could share the information with you.'

'Of course you did,' said Bristow, sarcastically. 'Who is this "Bugsy" character? Is he one of your contacts in the city gang?'

'No, he's my detective sergeant. We call him Bugsy because—'

DI Long cut him off. 'Who's the dead woman, Dawes? Why did you decide to electrocute her instead of shooting her?'

'Oh, so you've changed your mind about her being my mistress, then?' Jack was relieved.

'Not at all.' DI Long pressed him. 'She could still have been your mistress, up to her neck in your shady drugs operation. Or was she a CHIS?'

'A kiss?' asked Jack, momentarily confused. But Long was already clarifying.

'A Covert Human Intelligence Source. She could have turned on you — become a regular police informant, threatening to grass.'

'Did she bring the gun, intending to shoot you? Maybe she was scared of you and she brought it to defend herself,' insisted Bristow.

Before Jack could answer, DI Long pitched in again. 'What are you doing in Brightsea, anyway, Dawes?' She thrust her face into his. 'Were you planning to set up a network of operations here?'

'I'm on holiday with my wife.' During the onslaught of speculative questions, Jack could understand why some suspects confessed to a crime they hadn't committed, just to make it stop. They'd given him the duty solicitor who just sat there, scribbling notes. He hadn't even looked up, let alone offered legal advice. Jack knew his rights, even without an effective lawyer, but he appreciated that some people may not. 'I'd like a break now, please, and some food and drink. And if you don't want to face a charge of police misconduct due to harassment — and the rules are in PACE, if you need to look it up — I think you should use the time to speak to DCS Garwood.'

DI Long hesitated. It wouldn't hurt to speak to this Garwood bloke, just to be on the safe side. Mind you, he could be part of the corruption, too. It would certainly be a good collar if she could bag a crooked detective chief superintendent. She stood up. 'Interview suspended at—' she looked at her watch — 'five thirty.' She motioned to DC Nosworthy to turn off the audio equipment and they trooped out.

* * *

They put Jack in a police cell. He wondered what Corrie was doing and whether anyone had told her where he was. A fine holiday this was turning out to be. Hadn't he told her that holidays were a mistake, and you ended up wishing you'd never come? Maybe that was a bit unfair. Not everyone got arrested on holiday. Not in Brightsea and stone-cold sober, anyway. He looked around him. This was the first time he'd been inside a cell as a prisoner, instead of an arresting officer. Thoughtfully, he bit into the ham sandwich they'd brought him. Despite DI Long's browbeating interrogation, Jack had total faith in the justice system, of which he was an integral part. He accepted that in his case, it may take a while, but he had no doubt that the truth would eventually prevail. Without this firm conviction, he wouldn't have been able to do his job. He genuinely believed that if a person is innocent, they have nothing to fear.

He sipped his weak tea and wondered what Garwood would make of DI Long. He hoped his team would find some way to contact Corrie, before she did something rash. He knew how angry she'd be when she found out what had happened.

CHAPTER TEN

It was six o'clock and Garwood was at home, pruning his roses, when he received the call from DI Long. She had phoned Kings Richington station, asking for the DCS and emphasizing that it was an urgent and extremely important matter. Sergeant Parsloe had been putting on his coat to go home himself, when the switchboard asked if it was OK to give out Garwood's home number. Hearing that it was a detective inspector from the Brightsea constabulary, bells rang in Norman's head. That was where Jack and Mrs Dawes were spending their holiday. Maybe there'd been an accident. He hoped not. The DI said she would speak only to Garwood and it concerned a murder. With some trepidation, Parsloe instructed the officer on the switchboard to release the number.

* * *

'Detective Chief Superintendent Garwood? This is Detective Inspector Lorraine Long from Brightsea CID. I'm sorry to disturb you in the evening, sir, but I have a man in custody who claims he is one of your senior officers. I assumed that you would want to know without delay, so that you could either confirm his story or, as I suspect, refute it as a pathetic ruse to avoid any charges. Are you able to comment, sir?' She thought she'd better tread carefully, at least to start with. She had no evidence that this DCS was affiliated to any criminal group — but he might be. Best not to alert him of her suspicions.

Garwood was immediately cautious. Brightsea was where Dawes and his wife had booked into some expensive spa place. Mrs Garwood had been enthusing about it and even hinting that they might try it, too. It had to be Dawes that this DI had arrested. What the blazes had the man been up to now? He parried the question with one of his own. It was a subterfuge he had always found effective, since it actively avoided an immediate and possibly ill-advised response that he would regret later. 'Why hasn't your DCS contacted me about this, Inspector?'

Good question, she thought, *and I have a good answer. Because he doesn't know about it, yet.* She had no intention of sharing this case with her DCS until she'd cracked open the whole corrupt organization. She didn't want top brass taking all the credit, like they always did. If it was a straight competition between brains and braid, she knew what the outcome would be. 'I thought it better to establish the facts before informing him, sir.'

Clever, thought Garwood. It called for another question on his part, some more stalling while he thought hard. 'I see. What's the name of this man you have in custody?'

'Initially, he said it was Rupert Dawes and he was an electrician. Then, during questioning, he claimed he was known as Jack, and that he was a detective inspector in the Met's Murder Investigation Team. Personally, I think it's all a pack of lies designed to prevaricate, while his criminal associates find a way to get him released.'

Garwood groaned inwardly. Bloody Dawes! What was the man playing at? He knew they practised bloody silly, weird treatments at these health spa places, but he didn't think they gave out hallucinogenic drugs. Dawes must definitely be on something mind-bending. He decided it was safer not to admit to knowing him, until he knew what the disadvantages might be. 'What offence do you suspect this man has committed?'

'Murder, sir. And he doesn't have an alibi.'

She explained about the unidentified 'lady in black' and Dawes's part in finding the body. Then she told him about the gun they'd found in the pool next to the body, and the identical image on Jack's phone. When she described its connection to organized crime, every atom of self-preservation in Garwood's body oscillated with unease. He didn't seriously believe Dawes was capable of murder — did he? Then again, how well did you know anybody? The man had always been rebellious, making his own decisions and ignoring the rules. If there was any truth in this woman's suspicions, it could reflect very badly on him as DCS. A rogue officer in his team that he hadn't seen fit to root out could scupper any chance of promotion, never mind his aspirations of a knighthood. He needed to speak to Sir Barnaby, and quickly, before the proverbial hit the fan.

'I need to make some enquiries. Leave it with me, Inspector.' He terminated the call, leaving DI Long still without a definitive answer to her question. But from his terse responses, she was pretty sure DCS Garwood did know Dawes, and he was just covering his arse until he could safely pass the buck. The 'enquiries' he referred to could well mean he wanted to warn others in the OCG.

* * *

'Who was that, George?' Cynthia had come in, just at the end of the conversation. Being a little hard of hearing, Garwood always put the phone on speaker, so she'd overheard most of it.

'Nobody important, my dear.'

'It sounded pretty important to me. What did she mean, "murder" and "he doesn't have an alibi"? Who doesn't?'

71

'It's nothing that need concern you, and I wish you wouldn't listen in to confidential police matters.'

'If they take place in my home, I have every right to listen in. She was talking about Jack, wasn't she? I heard her mention his name. What's happened?'

Garwood cursed. The woman had ears like a bat! If he wanted any supper, he'd have to explain. 'That fancy hotel and spa, where Dawes and his wife have gone for a holiday — it seems they've found a woman's body, murdered, in a whirlpool.'

'Don't tell me they think Jack did it.' Cynthia burst out laughing.

'It's all very well to laugh, Cynthia, but we all have one murder in us, given sufficient provocation.'

'Yes, but not Jack. Corrie must think it's a hoot. I'll give her a ring.' She bit her lip. 'Oh, I can't. Carlene persuaded her not to take her phone, so she'd relax and wouldn't keep ringing in for a progress report on the business. I'll speak to Jack instead.' She picked up her phone and began to tap in his number.

'I don't think you will, Cynthia. Dawes has been arrested and he's in a police cell. They took his phone away.'

'But that's ridiculous! What are you going to do about it, George?'

'There's very little I can do. The crime has taken place outside my jurisdiction.'

'You're a chief superintendent. Surely you can pull a few strings?'

He assumed a pious expression. 'String-pulling isn't part of my job description, Cynthia. This has to be handled strictly according to the book.'

'Bollocks!' exclaimed Cynthia. 'You've pulled more strings than Jimi Hendrix, when it's suited you. It's obviously a terrible mistake by a DI trying to claw her way up the ladder at Jack's expense. Corrie is my best friend. Promise me you'll sort it out.'

Garwood capitulated for the sake of some peace and quiet. 'I'll telephone Sir Barnaby. I can't promise more than that.'

* * *

As it turned out, the conversation with Sir Barnaby was disappointing, not to say unsettling. Contrary to Garwood's expectations, the commander did not share his view that Dawes was somehow to blame and should, accordingly, be hung out to dry. Aware that Jack was responsible for the major successes of the MIT, and accordingly, the excellent reputation that it had earned, Sir Barnaby had a different suggestion.

'Here's what you do, Garwood. Contact an officer of equivalent rank in the National Crime Agency. Nobody's been charged with the shooting of the police officer in the drugs raid, yet, but I'm pretty sure the NCA will have a good idea who it was, even if they can't prove it yet. Find out who they suspect and get a description to the SIO in charge of Jack's murder case. The man they're looking for could well be hiding out at this Now to Zen place, where the gun has turned up. Two birds with one stone — you get Dawes released and the real killer put behind bars. Use your initiative, Garwood. Get on with it, man.'

Sir Barnaby wondered whether he should have spent more time spelling out his instructions — Garwood had never been the sharpest knife in the drawer — but he was in a hurry. He was late for a rare round of golf with his old friend, Sir Reginald, a man he frequently envied. Reggie was a very successful businessman. He had a big house, a lovely wife and, most of the time, his two sons ran the business, so he was able to take time off for a game of golf, any time he liked. He and Sir Barnaby had been knighted at around the same time — Sir Barnaby for his services to law and order and Sir Reginald for his work with various charities. It had been on the board of trustees of a police charity that they had met and become firm friends. Barnaby made a mental note to ensure Lobelia had invited Reggie and his wife to their next dinner party.

Garwood returned to his floribundas in a state of high agitation. This Dawes business had become serious and he wanted to distance himself from it, as quickly as possible. He had grave doubts about contacting the NCA, with whom he'd had less than convivial relationships in the past. In his opinion, they were far too keen on law enforcement and catching criminals, and didn't pay enough attention to the potential risks to a person's career prospects, especially someone hoping for early retirement and needing to maximize his pension. He would give it a great deal of thought before doing anything hasty. All that was needed was some masterly inactivity. With any luck, it would sort itself out without him having to do anything at all. In his experience, things had a habit of doing just that.

* * *

After George had gone back to his roses, Cynthia phoned Carlene, who was finishing off the dinner party order for Lady Lobelia Featherstonehaugh, Commander Sir Barnaby's wife. She had to keep reminding herself that it was pronounced 'Fanshawe'. When she heard what had happened to Jack, she was as unconvinced as Cynthia.

'That's total cobblers! Inspector Jack would never get involved in anything even slightly shifty, never mind murder. He's as straight as a die. How is Mrs D coping?'

'I don't know,' said Cynthia. 'She hasn't got her phone, so I can't contact her.'

'Oh shit! I made her leave it behind, so she could chill, without worrying about the Cuisine. It seemed like a good idea at the time. Is Mr Garwood going down to sort it out?'

'I doubt it,' said Cynthia. 'George says it must be handled "through the proper channels" which means fannying about until someone higher up the food chain takes responsibility. He's spoken to Sir Barnaby. I listened in and what he suggested seemed like a good idea to me, but I don't think George intends to do it yet.'

'That's no use. It could be too late if we don't do something now. We can't let Inspector Jack go to court, charged with murder. He won't get bail for such a serious offence, he'll end up on remand.'

'I agree. I think we should get down there and help Corrie. You know — the Three Cs, back together again?' In a crisis, Cynthia tended to regress to the language of her entitled childhood, where everything was 'spiffing' and crooks got a 'jolly good telling-off'. 'I'll ring the spa and book us in.'

When she finally got through to a beleaguered reception desk, after holding on through endless repeats of *The Four Seasons*, Cynthia got a recorded message saying that the Now to Zen had been temporarily closed by the police. This was due to an unfortunate incident, and nobody was allowed in or out. So now there was no chance of booking a room or being put through to Corrie. Cynthia relayed this to Carlene, who had already packed a bag and handed over management of the catering to her partner, Antoine, French chef and co-worker at her bistro, Chez Carlene.

Carlene was her usual pragmatic self. 'OK, so we'll stay in another hotel. There are loads of 'em along the Brightsea seafront. We can contact Mrs D when we get there.'

'How, if the police won't let us in or Corrie out, and the phone lines are shut down?'

'Dunno. I'll think of a way when I see the set-up.'

* * *

Reluctantly, DCS Garwood conceded that even if he'd put off ringing the NCA, he should brief the MIT of the current situation with regard to DI Dawes. What he definitely did not want to happen was that they got wind of it from another, less circumspect source. Their loyalty to Dawes was such that he wouldn't put it past them to start inquiries of their own to prove his innocence. He needed to impress upon them that they must let the law take its course. Any attempt to interfere would be summarily dealt with. He'd already found a note from Cynthia on the drinks' cabinet, where she knew he'd find it. It had read: *Gone to do your job for you. Back when we've caught the real killer.* What he needed to do now was make sure the MIT didn't have similar aspirations.

When the door opened and Garwood came in, the team fell silent and stood up, half-suspecting what was coming. Bugsy had confessed to them that he'd probably got the guvnor into hot water by emailing him an image of an 'iffy' gun. Then he'd unwittingly spoken about it to a copper on the Brightsea force. He was about to find out just how hot the water had become.

Garwood gestured to the team to sit down, then strutted to the front of the room. 'It pains me to have to inform you that Detective Inspector Dawes has placed himself in a most compromising position. During his stay at the Now to Zen Hotel and Spa with Mrs Dawes, a murder was committed. The dead woman has yet to be identified, but the Brightsea CID believe she was known to DI Dawes. This, together with other strong evidence linking him to police corruption, was sufficient for him to be arrested, and he is currently in custody.'

There were loud jeers of disbelief and concern. Garwood continued.

'He has yet to be charged but the SIO investigating the case is confident that this is imminent. I must emphasize, most strongly, that Kings Richington MIT cannot become involved in any way, however much we may want to. Any attempt to do so will be treated as misconduct and dealt with severely, through the issue of Reg 15 disciplinary notices. In the meantime, Sergeant Malone will continue as Acting Detective Inspector until a replacement for DI Dawes can be assigned.' He walked out before anyone could ask awkward questions.

Immediately, there was uproar.

'Are they mad, the Brightsea coppers?' demanded Aled. 'The boss wouldn't murder anyone.'

'And as for accusations of police corruption, nobody could be more honest than our DI.' Gemma was indignant at the very idea. So were the others on the team.

'The whole thing stinks.'

'It's probably one of their lot, and they're looking for a scapegoat.'

'I don't believe a word of it.'

Bugsy had not reacted until now. He stood up. 'It's my fault they think the guv is involved in police corruption. It'll be that email I sent with the image of the gun, connected to organized crime. It was used to wound a police officer in a drugs raid and now they think Jack wiped off the prints and chucked it in the whirlpool.'

'What are we going to do, Sarge? We can't just sit around doing nothing, like the old man wants us to.' Aled's comment was greeted by a bombardment of noisy agreement.

'As for that crack about, "however much we may want to get involved",' said DC Mitchell, 'who's he kidding? Garwood has no intention of getting involved. He's written off the boss already.'

'I take it the general consensus is that we do Brightsea's job for them and find out who killed the dead woman,' said Bugsy. 'I've thought of several lines of inquiry we could follow. It'll probably mean suspension, if we're caught. Hands up who's in?'

'Me!' It was unanimous.

CHAPTER ELEVEN

'Has anybody seen David?' Rainbow was feeling slightly guilty that she had given up on him. He obviously had issues, even if they weren't the ones he believed them to be. Since she had dismissed him so summarily, he hadn't been seen in the dining rooms or any of the other communal areas. He hadn't responded any of the times that she'd tapped on his door. She went to ask Meredith at reception.

'Has David checked out? I didn't get his surname.'

'That's because he didn't want to give one. Some of them don't, particularly men on their own. Apparently, it isn't manly to have facials and depilatory treatments. And in answer to your question, nobody has checked out. The police are still keeping us all locked in. Unless it's an emergency, like appendicitis. Even then, I expect you have to be handcuffed to a constable while you're on the operating table.'

'That means David must be here somewhere.'

'I guess so.'

Rainbow was pensive. 'He's a complex young man. Do you think he's here for something other than spiritual guidance?'

'Like what?'

'I don't know. What did he put down as his occupation?'

Meredith fetched it up on the computer. 'He's a window cleaner.'

Rainbow laughed. 'I don't think so. If he is, I bet he's a lousy one. His aura was that of a critical thinker, an introvert with deep analytical abilities. I didn't see a bucket and squeegee.'

'Really?' Meredith was thoughtful. 'I wonder if he lied about anything else?'

* * *

Corrie had a plan. She desperately needed to get some kind of message to Jack, to let him know she was going to get him out — although she hadn't a clue how. But first things first. If Jack couldn't come to her, she'd go to him. There were two uniformed constables guarding the front and back entrances. She felt sorry for what she was about to do, but needs must.

'I insist you let me pass. I have to see my husband.'

The first constable, who looked about fourteen and still had acne, put out an arm to restrain her. 'I'm sorry, madam, we're under strict instructions not to let anyone leave until DI Long approves it.'

Corrie took a deep breath. 'Well, I say "bum" to your DI Long. She has no right to keep us all here.'

The other constable looked shocked. 'Well, actually, yes she has. There's been a murder and she won't allow anyone to leave the scene until she's finished her investigation and charged the killer. You see, there will be witness statements to be taken, and at the moment, nobody is coming forward and helping with her inquiries.'

'That's rubbish. She doesn't even know who the dead woman is, let alone who killed her. It could take months. I don't see why we should suffer because of her incompetence. Now, are you going to let me out or not?'

'No, and I must ask you to calm yourself down, or—'

Corrie stamped on his foot.

'Oww!' He hopped about. 'That's an assault on a police officer in the execution of his duty. You can get six months for that.'

Corrie did it again.

'Right, that's it. Now it's a sustained and repeated assault with a significant degree of premeditation. I shall have to arrest you.'

The other constable was talking on his radio. 'They're sending a car for her.'

* * *

Sitting alone in his cell, Jack wondered how much of an extension DI Long had negotiated to the hours she was allowed to hold him without charge. He was pretty sure she *would* charge him, when the time ran out. Dispassionately, he would have to agree that she had a reasonable case, had he not known he was innocent.

He took a couple of forkfuls of the stew they'd brought him — at least, he thought it was stew — then pushed it to one side. Used, as he was, to food cooked by a top-class caterer, prison food tasted pretty dreadful. On the other hand, he reckoned it would probably taste equally dreadful to blokes who lived on burgers and pizza.

He had no illusions about Garwood putting his neck on the line for him. He doubted Garwood would put his neck on the line for his own mother, if a promotion was at risk. What Jack couldn't know was that the cavalry — in the form of the MIT and the Three Cs — would soon come galloping over the metaphorical horizon to rescue him.

* * *

When Corrie arrived at the station, she expected to be processed and charged with assaulting a police officer. She knew the routine. Instead, she was taken to an interview room and given a cup of tea. DC Nosworthy stood by the door. He smiled at her but didn't speak.

DI Long swept in, laptop under her arm, and sat down opposite Corrie. Without preamble, she asked, 'How long has your husband been involved in organized crime?'

Corrie put down her cup. 'Now, if you're going to be silly, Lorraine, we aren't going to get any further forward, are we? Jack isn't, and never has been, involved in anything corrupt, and if you'd done your background checks properly, you'd already know that.'

DI Long blinked. 'I don't need you to tell me my job, Mrs Dawes.'

'Well, apparently you do. Have you identified the dead woman yet?'

'I think I'll ask the questions—'

'So, that'll be a "no", then. You see, what I'd do, in your position, is ask myself why a woman of obviously reduced circumstances would turn up dead in an expensive place like the Now to Zen. My answer would be that she had arranged to meet someone — a person she was threatening in some way. It'll be someone who has a lot to lose and who killed her, in order to shut her up. Once you find out who that person is, you're halfway to identifying the dead woman and the motive for her murder. It isn't rocket science, if you think it through, instead of jumping to obvious conclusions. As a detective inspector, you should have learned by now that the obvious is very rarely the truth. But, you see, while you're focusing all your efforts on Jack, the murderer will be planning his escape. For all we know, he may have legged it already.'

DI Long could feel the initiative slipping away. She was also aware of DC Nosworthy disguising a snigger with a cough, behind her back. 'If your husband is innocent, like you say, how do you explain this?' DI Long spun her laptop around and showed Corrie a photograph of the gun that had been emailed to Jack's phone.

'Well, that's pretty simple, when you know Jack. He saw the gun in the whirlpool, when we found the body. He thought he recognized it from the CCTV of a drugs raid and phoned MIT to ask Sergeant Malone to check it out and email him a photo.'

'Sergeant Malone — would that be "Bugsy" Malone?'

'That's right, Lorraine. Now you're getting it. Jack was just trying to help your investigation along with a piece of useful information. Which was naughty, really, because we were supposed to be on holiday. Can I see him, please?'

DI Long decided against it. Despite his wife's plausible explanation, she was reluctant to accept any alternative to what seemed like a watertight case against Dawes. Added to which, she didn't have any other suspects. At this stage, she didn't think collusion with his wife was a good idea. 'Not yet. Not until I've made further inquiries.'

'Are you going to put me in a cell?' Corrie planned to shout to Jack once she was in the custody suite.

Ever suspicious, DI Long decided it would be safer to take Corrie back to the Now to Zen and keep her there, as far away from the suspect as possible. 'No. Just think yourself lucky I've decided not to press assault charges. I accept that you were stressed, when you committed the offence.'

DC Nosworthy escorted Corrie to the waiting police car. He whispered to her as he bent to put a hand over her head, to guide her in. 'Don't worry, Mrs Dawes. I'll tell your husband you were here.' Noz had never really believed in Jack's guilt. As a detective constable, it was his job to follow orders, but he reckoned the DI had made up her mind, regardless of police procedure, and that couldn't be right, could it?

* * *

Cynthia and Carlene arrived in a taxi at the Stone's Throw, a modest hotel dwarfed by the magnificent Now to Zen next door. It was named because it was literally just a stone's throw from the beach and the sea. As luck would have it, they climbed from the taxi just as Corrie was being escorted out of the police car. Carlene spotted her immediately and dashed round to speak to her, but the officers had already hurried Corrie inside.

'Yoo-hoo! Mrs D!' Carlene shouted, waving her hands, but the constables standing guard on the door moved her on. She ran back to where Cynthia stood looking up at the windows of the spa.

'Bugger! I was too late,' gasped Carlene.

'No, you weren't,' said Cynthia. 'She heard you. Look!'

Corrie was on the fourth floor, waving back through the blue-tinted panoramic window. There was a balcony outside where guests could sit and watch the tide, buffeting the shore. It was one of the therapies. Corrie drew back the sliding door and ventured out onto the balcony.

'I'm so pleased to see you,' she shouted, but her words were carried away on the wind.

'We've come to help,' Carlene yelled back. 'This is barmy. We can't hold a proper conversation like this. Gimme your phone, Mrs Garwood. I'll go round to the front entrance and ask the coppers to give it to Mrs D.'

'Didn't you bring Corrie's phone with you?' asked Cynthia.

'No. I didn't know where it was and besides, I wasn't going to let myself into her house and start rummaging through her stuff, was I? Gimme yours.'

Cynthia handed it over and Carlene ran round to the Now to Zen. She was back, minutes later. 'They radioed the woman in charge and she said no.'

DI Long hadn't wanted Corrie talking to anybody outside the hotel. She still wasn't convinced that she wasn't up to something. She didn't know what, but she was taking no chances. This was the wife of her main suspect — her only suspect. She had been plausible, but then so had Dawes. They could be into serious crime together. It wouldn't be the first time a married couple had been found guilty of corruption and murder by joint enterprise.

'Right,' said Carlene, judging the distance from the ground to the open window. 'Give me a leg-up onto that wall.'

Cynthia hoisted her up. 'What are you going to do?' You never knew with Carlene.

'I'm going to chuck your phone in through that window.'

'What if you miss?'

'Then Mr Garwood will have to buy you another one, won't he?'

'Are you sure you can throw that far? What if you lose your balance?' Cynthia was more concerned about Carlene falling off the wall than for the safety of her phone.

'I won't.' She rolled up her sleeves. 'Mrs D! Catch!' She did a discus-like wind-up and hurled it.

It sailed through the air and in through the window, like a heat-seeking missile. Corrie leaped in the air and grabbed it before it hit the floor. She hadn't been captain of the Lady Agatha's Academy for Girls' netball team for nothing.

'Right, now, Mrs Garwood.' Carlene climbed down off the wall and pulled out her own phone. 'What's your mobile number? I'll ring Mrs D.'

Cynthia looked blank. 'I haven't a clue. I mean, how many people know their own mobile number?'

Carlene rolled her eyes. 'What do you do when you have to give it to somebody?'

'I take out my phone and read the number. I can't do that if I haven't got it, can I?'

Fortunately, Corrie knew Carlene's number and had punched it into Cynthia's phone the minute she caught it. 'I'm so glad you guys are here. Jack's been arrested for murder. He's in a police cell.'

'Yes, we know.' Carlene was eager to get started. 'That's why we're here. We can get things moving on the outside, while you keep your eyes and ears open on the inside. Between us, we're going to crack this and get Inspector Jack out of the slammer.'

Cynthia took over the phone. 'Barnaby suggested to George that he get in touch with the NCA to see if they have a suspicion as to who had used the gun in the whirlpool to shoot that copper. They probably know exactly who it was, but they haven't been able to nail him. Only I don't think George is keen to do it.'

Carlene grabbed the phone back. 'I'm going to ring Sergeant Bugsy. He'll do it. He's got mates in all sorts of places. He's bound to have a contact in the NCA. When we get a description or maybe even an e-fit, if we're lucky, I'll email it to you. You can see if it matches anyone in the spa.'

'Brilliant idea, Carlene. That old sourpuss DI Long is convinced it's Jack, so she isn't even looking for anyone else. I'm equally convinced that the killer is still in this hotel.'

'Hurrah!' trilled Cynthia. 'Three cheers for the Three Cs! We're on the case, girls!'

Corrie heaved a sigh. 'Cyn?'

'Yes, Corrie?'

'I'm very glad you're here — but do give it a rest.'

CHAPTER TWELVE

'Clive, what have you got for me?' Bugsy stood behind the digital forensics specialist and looked at the screen over his shoulder.

'I hacked into the National Crime Agency site and after a lot of trawling, I eventually found reports of the drugs raid where the officer was shot. There's the CCTV footage, obviously, of the County Lines operation, working out of London and into Kings Richington, but details of the organized crime group are sparse. I'm guessing the NCA case is still wide open and they're unwilling to reveal too much, digitally, until they've rounded up the gang and caught the bloke who fired the gun.'

'No chance of a picture of him, I suppose?'

'None at all, Sarge. They were all in black with bala-clavas and the footage is fogged, at best. Could be anyone.'

Bugsy's phone rang. 'Hello, Carlene, love. How are you doing?'

'I'm in Brightsea, Sergeant Bugsy. Me and Mrs Garwood have come down to help Mrs D get Inspector Jack out of jail.'

'That's a coincidence. The MIT are working on the same thing. We know he isn't guilty, same as you. What have you got?'

'Mrs Garwood overheard Sir Barnaby telling Mr Garwood to contact the NCA. He said although they haven't yet been able to charge anyone with the shooting, they would have a pretty good idea who it was, and Mr Garwood should get a description to the SIO running Inspector Jack's murder case. He reckoned the man they were looking for could well be one of the guests hiding out at this Now to Zen place, where the gun turned up.'

'Right. That's unusually perceptive of the commander. When did the DCS say he was going to do it?'

'He didn't. Not exactly. That's why I'm ringing you. Mrs Garwood says he's putting it off, hoping someone else will take responsibility, in case it goes tits up.'

'In that case, it's down to me. I'm used to things going tits up. It's the story of my life. I've got an old drinking buddy in the NCA, who worked on the County Lines case when they were peddling drugs into Kings Richington. I'll call in a favour.'

Carlene was cautious. 'If we get anything, we'd better not share it with the SIO, though. Mrs D says she's determined Inspector Jack's guilty and won't listen to anything else. She's going to charge him, so we need to be quick.'

'I'm on it, love. I'll get back to you ASAP. Don't do anything dangerous.'

Carlene grinned. 'When have you ever known me do anything dangerous?'

'Not in the last ten minutes, while you've been talking to me, but otherwise . . .'

* * *

'Charlie? It's me, Bugsy Malone. How's it going?'

'Bugsy, good to hear from you. Time we met for a few pints and a catch-up.'

'Yeah, let's do that. But what I'm really after is some info on one of your targets.' Bugsy reminded him of the circumstances of the raid, the Taurus Model 856 that was used, and the bloke the NCA believed pulled the trigger. 'Even though you haven't put anyone in the frame for it, I'm betting you guys have a good idea who it is.'

Charlie hesitated. 'Yeah, we do, but we're having to box a bit clever on this one, Bugsy. We want to get the whole group, especially the boss. In this game, it's not so much who pulled the trigger, it's who paid for the bullet. We nicked a couple of 'em during the raid, but they're too scared to grass, even in prison. The others got away. Chummy with the gun disappeared off the scene, taking all the money. He could have escaped abroad. Although we issued all-ports warnings at the time, they have ways of getting round it. This is a vicious gang that punishes anyone who double-crosses them. At the moment, it's a toss-up who gets to him first — us or the OCG. He'd better hope it's us.'

'My problem, Charlie, is that my guvnor has been fingered for a murder on the basis that he recognized the gun, and thanks to me, he was arrested with a picture of it on his phone. It turned up where he's staying with his wife on holiday, in a hotel and spa in Brightsea. They found it in a whirlpool, next to a dead woman.'

'Blimey! So you're thinking that the geezer we're looking for could have killed her, then chucked it in there?'

'If you can give me a name and a description, we could both get a result. There's a good chance he's lying low inside the spa hotel.'

'If it's who we think it is, his name's Eddie "Coke" Clayton. Six-foot-two, slim build, aged around forty. Last time anyone saw him, he was rocking a Van Dyke beard and moustache to cover an old scar from a knife attack. Course, he could have shaved it off by now.'

'Coke?'

'Yeah. The sort you shove up your nose, not the kind you drink from cans. Eddie Clayton was the "Cocaine King". He even got his wife hooked on it.'

'There's a Mrs Cocaine King?'

'Yep. Della Clayton — an American, now believed to be living in London. Suspected of prostitution, theft and drugs, thanks to Eddie. Never enough evidence to arrest her, so no prints or DNA. He left her to face the music when he took off with the assets.'

'Nice bloke.' Bugsy reckoned whatever happened to this creep, he deserved it. 'Don't suppose you've got a description of her?'

'I can do better than that. I've got a mugshot on file. We put a tail on her for a while, hoping she'd lead us to Eddie, but she never did. Last known address is Braxton Tower, a dingy twenty-storey tower block in East London.'

'Is she still there?'

'No. She did a "moonlight" and we lost her. Are you thinking she's in this spa hotel with Eddie?'

'Anything's possible, Charlie. Send me the mugshot. I'll let you know straight away if we find either of them.'

'If you catch Clayton, the beers are on me.'

'I'll hold you to that, mate.'

'Watch yourself, Bugsy. When the mob catch up with chummy — and they will — it'll be nasty, and you don't want to be caught in the crossfire.'

* * *

Having got a name, Clive used all his forensic sleuthing genius to trace Eddie 'Coke' Clayton. The man was clearly a career racketeer, in a crime group with a reputation for cutting off fingers with bolt cutters and nailing victims to garage doors. His appearance had changed drastically several times over the last ten years, and even Clive couldn't come up with anything definitive.

'He's fallen off the radar since the drugs raid, disappeared from all the usual sources of identification. If he has a passport, it'll be a forgery. He has so many aliases, it's hard to tell which one he's using now, but it won't be Eddie Clayton.'

Bugsy emailed everything they had to Carlene. 'I don't know if Mrs Dawes will be able to clock this bloke, but tell her to be careful — he's dangerous.'

'I'll warn her, Sergeant Bugsy, and I'll get back to you as soon as I've got anything to report.'

* * *

Corrie, Carlene and Cynthia were now able to hold video calls from within their respective hotels. It made communication much more effective. The Now to Zen was still cordoned off while teams of police officers took endless statements, mainly focused on what people had observed of Jack Dawes, particularly any suspicious activity.

'What we need you to do, Mrs D, is clock all the blokes around forty, just over six foot tall and who may or may not have a beard and moustache.'

'Well, that shouldn't take long,' said Corrie. 'There aren't many men here on their own — most of 'em have been dragged here by their wives, like Jack.'

'Hang on,' chipped in Cynthia. 'According to what the NCA told Bugsy, our man has a wife. She may be there with him, in which case we're looking for a married couple.'

'And from what I can gather, they won't be getting on too well. He escaped with all the money from the raid and left her behind to face the gang. They might both be at the Now to Zen waiting for the heat to die down. Is there anyone like that?' asked Carlene.

'One couple fits that description, including the beard and moustache, and they've done nothing but row since they got here,' said Corrie. 'But the thing is, he stormed off in the middle of dinner the first night we arrived. I'm not sure if it was before or after the murder, but if it's Timothy and Miriam Bennett, he's already got away. Miriam's still here, though. What do you know about the wife?'

'We've got a pic of her, Mrs D. I'll send it — stand by.' Carlene pinged across the picture of Della Clayton. When

Corrie didn't reply for some moments, Carlene wondered what had gone wrong. 'Have you got it? Do you recognize her?'

Corrie took a deep breath. 'Oh crikey! Yes, I recognize her, all right. That's the dead woman we found in the whirlpool.'

'Flippin' heck!' exclaimed Carlene. 'That means the bloke we're looking for is probably still there. He topped his wife, somehow, dumped the incriminating gun and now he's waiting for Inspector Jack to be charged, so he can disappear again.'

'Doesn't that let Jack off the hook, now we've identified the dead woman?' asked Cynthia.

'Not really,' said Corrie. 'DI Long will argue that she came here to meet Jack, a fellow gang member, demanding her share of the money, and he let her in and killed her. If anything, her turning up here makes Jack look even more guilty. I don't think we should tell DI Long that we know who the dead woman is — not yet anyway. We don't want to make things worse for Jack.'

'I still don't understand how she got in, if security there is so tight,' said Carlene. 'None of the guests would have been allowed to smuggle her in. They'd have been spotted and asked what they were up to. It's an expensive place. You can't let folks in for free.'

'I've been thinking about that, and I believe I can hazard a guess,' Corrie offered. 'When we first arrived, before everybody was locked down, I was looking out of the window, watching the security men check everybody in and out of the front entrance. There was a black cat waiting patiently for the door to open so it could sneak inside. It waited until there was a bit of an altercation between the doorman and a guest when being asked for identity, and the cat took the opportunity to nip inside. Neither the guest nor the doorman noticed it.'

'But you did,' commented Cynthia.

'Oh yes. I reckon Della Clayton bought herself a cheap black tunic and trousers and slipped in at ten thirty, when the security man was letting Timothy Bennett out. The girls here all look the same in uniform with their hair tied back in a bun. She could have slipped past him and he simply didn't notice her. Tim Bennett was pretty drunk and making a lot of noise. It was a gamble, but her reason for wanting to get in must have been important enough for her to risk it.'

'We need to get this information to Sergeant Bugsy,' decided Carlene. 'He'll tell us what to do next.'

CHAPTER THIRTEEN

David had spent long hours studying the Now to Zen databases and now he was certain the malicious code being used to steal money from several sites originated from Brightsea. The number of staff with access to the database, or even with sufficient knowledge to be able to do it, was limited, which narrowed down the search considerably. It would be unethical and bad practice to start accusing people without proof, so he was unsure how to proceed. The murder, and the turmoil it had caused throughout the hotel, had impinged only slightly on his consciousness. He was contemplating his next step when a typed note was pushed under his door. He picked it up and opened the door to see who had left it, but there was nobody there.

It read, *I understand why you're here. I want to help you. Meet me tonight at ten o'clock by the rooftop swimming pool.*

David looked at it for several minutes. He guessed it could mean one of two things. Either the person who wrote it — and he hoped it was Rainbow — had acknowledged his self-confessed social awkwardness and this was to be an assignation to help him to conquer it. Or someone had discovered his real purpose for being there, and was prepared to

give him some inside information. In either case, he decided
he would go.

* * *

'Sergeant Bugsy, it's her. The dead woman in the whirlpool,
it's Della Clayton. Mrs D recognized her from the mugshot.'
Carlene was anxious for some guidance on what they should
do next.

'Right, love. To recap what we already know from
the NCA, Eddie Clayton and his wife, Della, were active
members of an OCG. During a particularly profitable operation, Eddie shot a copper, so he needed to vanish, and a bit
smartish. He took most of the cash with him, leaving Della, a
heavy cocaine user, behind to face the gang. Knowing Eddie
was a double-crossing little weasel, they accepted her story
that he'd double-crossed her too, and she genuinely didn't
know where he'd gone, but the interrogation must have been
pretty nasty. I reckon he left the country and kept his head
down, but he didn't dare try to smuggle the cash out with
him, so he stashed it here in the UK. When he came back to
get it, Della somehow tracked him down and demanded her
share of the loot or she'd shop him — either to the gang, or
to us, or both.'

'Well, we know she didn't blag her way into the Now to
Zen to meet Inspector Jack, which is what the local cops will
believe when they find out who she is. What we have to do is
find the bloke she really did come to see — this Eddie Clayton.'

'Dead right,' said Bugsy. 'And I bet a pound to a penny
he's still in the hotel. He knows if the gang finds him, he's
a dead man.'

'At the moment, it's the safest place for him, because
it's crawling with cops,' agreed Carlene. 'But Mrs D says
there are several blokes staying there who could be him from
the description, especially if he's shaved off the face fungus.
We don't know what name he's using. She can't go round
interrogating them all.'

'There's a saying among us detectives — never show your hand until you've established the relative position of your arse to your elbow. There's a trick she could try. It's a bit of a gamble, but I know the guv's wife will be up for it. She must be desperate to get Jack cleared.'

'We all are. What's the trick?' Carlene was keen for action.

'She gets one of the staff on her side, maybe bungs him a few quid, and gets him to go all around the hotel, wherever groups of inmates — I mean, guests — congregate. He calls out, "Urgent message for Eddie Clayton from his wife, Della." It won't force chummy out into the open, he's too smart for that, but he'll realize someone has identified the dead woman, and with any luck, it'll scare him into some kind of knee-jerk reaction.'

'I get it. Good plan, Sergeant Bugsy. We're on it.' Carlene hurried off to share the intel with the other two Cs.

After he finished the call with Carlene, Bugsy was uneasy. He knew how dangerous these gangs were and he wasn't at all happy about the three women in Brightsea getting involved. What if Eddie found out that Mrs Dawes was behind the message to flush him out? He had tortured and killed people, including women, for much less. It wouldn't end well. He resolved to go down there himself.

* * *

'Did you get all that, Mrs D?' Patience had never been one of Carlene's virtues and she was glad to be doing something at last, even if it was only to pass on Bugsy's suggestion.

'Yes, thanks, Carlene. Sounds like a plan. I'll do it in the morning, when everyone's having breakfast. Cyn's phone is low on battery and I don't have a charger.' Corrie looked at her watch. It was quarter to ten. A bit late, but she thought she'd go down to reception. A smart place like this should have a charger they could loan to a guest. She made a mental note never again to go anywhere without her phone — it was like losing an arm.

When she got there, she found a different young lady at the desk.

'Hello,' said Corrie, brightly. 'No Penny or Meredith?'

'No, I'm afraid not. Mrs Hawkins has gone to sort out a menu problem in the kitchen and Meredith's on her break. How can I help? I hope it's nothing that needs me to go into the computer system, because frankly, I'm not very good at it. I'm a Zen buddy — Meredith and Mrs Hawkins do all the technical stuff.'

'I just need a charger for my phone. I didn't bring one with me.'

'Oh, that's fine.' She breathed a sigh of relief. 'I can cope with that, no problem.'

Corrie went back to her room with the charger, missing Jack and wishing she could just speak to him. How dare that Lorraine Long person put him in a cell! He was an honest, clever, first-rate detective inspector. Corrie couldn't wait to see how smart that frightful woman would look when the Three Cs found the real killer and she'd have to admit she got it all wrong.

* * *

David reached the rooftop swimming pool at exactly ten o'clock. There was no one there, so he sat down on one of the poolside seats to wait. The terrace and bar had excellent views over Brightsea and the seashore. Waves were crashing in, so he guessed it was high tide. It was very romantic. A clear sky with moon and stars — perfect for a late-night assignation. The only thing he found slightly disconcerting was the relatively flimsy safety rail. He got up and peered over the side. If anyone lost their balance and toppled over, he didn't give much for their chances. But then 'caution' was his middle name. No doubt it had been approved by the health-and-safety people. He decided he needed a bolder attitude to life, if he was ever to have any fun. Maybe, after he'd completed this assignment, he would move out from the tiny bedsit, just yards across the lane from his mother's house, and find himself a bachelor pad of some kind. He wasn't even sure such places were called that anymore, but it would give him the independence he craved. More importantly, he'd be able to entertain ladies without his mother watching out for them and 'popping in' with her cupcakes and curiosity.

It was while he was pondering on such matters that she arrived. Not Rainbow — Meredith.

'Hello, David. Thank you so much for coming.'

'Not at all.' He was rather disappointed. He'd hoped it would be Rainbow, come to ease him out of his crippling shyness with women. 'Your note said you know why I'm here and you can help me.'

She nodded. 'Rainbow told me she read your aura. She said it was predominantly the aura of a seeker of the truth, with a strong concern for rule-keeping and the law. That was despite the fact that when you booked in, you said you needed help with social anxiety.'

'Yes, well . . .'

'It's all right. I understand. You work for the Now to Zen Corporation, don't you?'

'Yes. How did you guess?'

'Oh, it wasn't a guess. The truth is, the hotel Wi-Fi in general has never been safe, by any means. The security is quite weak. Visitors often fall prey to hacks, data theft and third-party monitoring. All the sensitive information that you access and transmit using it can be easily tracked. That includes the history of your online searches. I'm the hotel's Wi-Fi admin and I've been looking at your internet history. You've been sent here to find out who's planting the malicious code and stealing money. It's no secret that the Brightsea Now to Zen has been leaking finances like a sieve.'

'That's right,' agreed David. 'And now it's spread to other sites. Do you know who's behind it?'

'Absolutely. I'll lose my job, of course.'

'Please, don't worry about that. I'm the senior UK software engineer for the Now to Zen Corporation. I'll tell the

US IT manager that it's thanks to you I've traced the code and stopped the leak. It'll make a huge difference to your future.'

She hesitated. 'All right. I'll tell you. It's Penny — Mrs Hawkins. She's been transferring money via a malware code for ages. She gambles, you see. Mostly online poker. She owes thousands. I think she was planning to stop once she'd stolen enough to pay her debts, but of course, that would never happen, would it? I mean, addicts can't stop. I feel sorry for Mr Hawkins. He doesn't have anything to do with IT. He won't have any idea what she's been doing, just that the hotel was losing money.'

David wasn't surprised. 'I was getting close. It had to be her — or you, frankly. You're the only two with enough knowledge and access to be able to do it. Well, thanks very much, Meredith. I'll report back to my boss.' He paused. 'Maybe I could buy you dinner, once this is over?'

'Thanks, David, that would be lovely.' She stood looking out at the seashore in the moonlight. 'It's beautiful here, isn't it?' She pointed. 'Look, you can see the pier if you lean over a bit. It's all lit up. It looks like Las Vegas at night.'

David leaned over the rail. 'I can't see it properly.'

'You need to lean a bit further.'

'Oh yeah. I can see it now.'

He was beginning to think he was finally conquering his shyness. Unfortunately for him, he never got the chance to find out. With his body already a fair way over the rail, Meredith simply grabbed his legs and tipped him over. He plummeted to the ground.

* * *

Penny Hawkins was in the kitchen discussing the vegan menu with the head chef. There had been complaints from someone who thought she had seen raw meat being delivered in a van, only yards behind one that was delivering vegetable and plant products. She was concerned that the person tasked with unloading the meat would have to pass through the vegetable preparation area to get to the meat refrigerators.

The chef was fiery and short-tempered. He wasn't the easiest of men to deal with on a good day and he didn't like criticism. 'Fine! Fine! Tell her I'll reorganize the entire layout of my kitchen in case any invisible vapours from the meat filter through the hermetically sealed packaging and into the atmosphere — despite the sophisticated, award-winning ventilation systems — and contaminate a lentil!'

One of the commis chefs, in an effort to avoid the chef's rant, had just dragged several large plastic sacks of food waste outside to the recycling area. There were several waiting to be taken away next day. He paused for a breath of air before going back inside. Seconds later, he heard something heavy fall from the sky and land on the waste sacks. He guessed it must be some sort of large bird, like a swan or goose. He opened the door to see, then shot back inside.

'Quick! Somebody call an ambulance!'

Everyone in the kitchen dashed outside. Penny recognized David straight away, his broken body sprawled, limp and motionless, across the black bags.

'Oh my goodness, this is terrible. I knew the poor man suffered with social anxiety, but I had no idea he was suicidal. He must have gone up to the rooftop pool and jumped off.' Penny wondered when all the ghastly troubles afflicting the hotel would end. Dick was right — she fully expected the Jefferson lawyers to move in and close them down.

The paramedics were on the scene in minutes, hastened by the police who were still securing the hotel. They examined the body, then made a surprising discovery.

'He isn't dead.' They moved quickly after that, setting up a drip and essential monitors, then transporting him very carefully into the ambulance parked outside the kitchens. The head chef wondered how long it would be before he received a complaint from the vegan lady about a human body lying too close to the vegetable preparation area.

CHAPTER FOURTEEN

Next morning, Meredith was behind the reception desk as usual when Rainbow appeared, anxious to impart some news.

'Isn't it awful? That poor young man. I blame myself.'

Meredith assumed a puzzled expression. 'Sorry, I don't understand. What young man? What's happened?'

'Haven't you heard? It's David. The guest with anxiety issues. He jumped off the roof last night.'

Meredith gasped. 'That's just terrible. He must have been so depressed.'

'I know,' said Rainbow. 'It's my fault. I read his aura and I should have seen it coming.'

'You mustn't blame yourself. He was a complicated man with hidden problems.'

'All the same, I might have been able to prevent it, if I hadn't dismissed him without a proper reading. But his aura gave every indication that he was a strong-minded seeker of truth, just not very good with people — especially women — although I think he wanted to be. And I never believed the window-cleaning nonsense. His feminine side was ablaze with colour, meaning he was focusing on his future and advancement in his profession. I wouldn't have expected that from a window cleaner, especially one contemplating suicide.'

'Never mind,' said Meredith. 'I guess you can't get it right every time.'

'Well, I'm certainly going to next time. I'll do a full aura analysis and find a way to build his confidence and self-esteem.'

This time, Meredith was genuinely puzzled. 'How will you do that, now he's passed on?'

Rainbow beamed. 'Oh, didn't I say? He isn't dead, thankfully, only badly injured. Heaps of kitchen sacks full of vegetable peelings broke his fall. Wasn't that incredibly lucky? I put it down to the bright red band of colour, arching above his head. It indicates survival, courage and determination. He's in the Jefferson hospital, unconscious, but they say he'll recover fully in time. I'll visit him as soon as they let us out of here.'

Meredith went white. She felt as though she might faint. It was luck, all right. The most astonishingly bad luck, for her. What were the odds on anyone surviving a fall like that? She needed time to think this through. How much time did she have before he regained consciousness and told everyone what had really happened?

* * *

Corrie had passed David the previous evening. He'd been on the way up to the rooftop pool and she'd been going back to her room with the charger she'd borrowed from reception. Later, she'd seen the ambulance from her window, and at the time, hadn't realized it was David they were taking away. The word going around at breakfast was that the lad had tried to commit suicide. As far as the police were concerned, he'd booked into the spa with self-acclaimed anxiety issues, which more or less confirmed it. They weren't investigating it as suspicious. The man was safe in hospital and unlikely or unable to make a second attempt, so now he was the responsibility of the appropriate agencies. They had enough on their plate with the dead woman in the pool.

Corrie thought about that. When she'd passed David, he'd smiled and she'd wished him good evening. Being a copper's wife, she noticed things. Jack always said she'd make an excellent witness. What she'd noticed on this occasion was that he was smartly dressed in a grey suit, and what looked like a crisp new shirt and silk tie. He certainly wasn't carrying any swimming togs. She also got a hint of a rather expensive men's *eau de parfum*. Hardly what you'd wear if you were about to end your life. More like the kind of thing a young man would wear to impress a young lady on a date.

She wondered if she should share her thoughts with someone. She wished Jack were here. But her priority was to consider her next move in her mission to free her husband, so she decided to ask Louis if he'd help her with the ploy to identify Eddie Clayton.

Louis was always game for a challenge and agreed readily. She explained that Clayton would have checked in under a false name. Her plan was that Louis would call out his real name and claim that he had a message about Della. Corrie would lurk somewhere close by and watch to see if any man of Clayton's description reacted.

'He won't identify himself, but he's bound to be surprised,' she explained.

'Why are we looking for this bloke, Corrie? Does he owe you money?'

'No, not me exactly. But he is holding a good deal of cash from illegal drug deals. He's wanted by the police for wounding a copper and by the gang he was working with for double-crossing them. I believe he was the one who killed his wife, Della — the woman we found dead in the whirlpool. I want him because he's the reason my husband has been wrongfully arrested for her murder and is sitting in a prison cell, unable to do it for himself.'

'Sound like good enough reasons to me,' Louis decided. 'They say the dead woman was a cocaine addict. Drugs are filthy. They ruin your mind and your body — psychosis and heart failure. No one sane would put that poison into a healthy body. Let's get him. Where d'you want to start?'

* * *

The Cheerful Chophouse was buzzing with folk getting the full English — eggs, bacon, sausage, mushrooms, black pudding, hash browns, tomatoes, baked beans and fried bread. As a chef, Corrie deemed it a cardiac arrest on a plate — but she conceded it was cheerful. As arranged, Louis strode to the centre of the room and shouted, 'Urgent message for Eddie Clayton about his wife, Della.' His stentorian voice had been honed on bellowed instructions to swimming classes, tennis lessons and 'Louis's Boot Camp', designed for guests who thought they were tough. The unfortunate effect was that everybody in the room looked up in surprise, including a few men of the hirsute persuasion.

Louis shrugged. 'That went well. They all reacted. What do we do now?'

'It's fine,' assured Corrie. 'The object of the exercise is to let him know we're on to him. It's what he does in response to that, that's important. Come on, let's do the other dining rooms.'

They repeated the performance in the Ritz Restaurant with a similar result. The Dorchester Room hummed with quiet conversation, while guests breakfasted on champagne with appropriately swanky food. Corrie noticed melting pains au chocolat, eggs benedict with smoked salmon and melon prosciutto skewers. In these hallowed surroundings, Louis delivered his message with rather less volume but still robustly.

Sitting alone at a table in the window, Sir Marcus Wellbeloved paused for barely a nanosecond, before breaking into his soft-boiled egg topped with caviar. A man in his position needed to be on high alert, ready to respond to any threat, if he were to stay alive. He had, accordingly, observed Louis and Corrie entering the dining room together and wondered what they were up to. Now, he knew. It was time to go.

* * *

DI Long was aware that she couldn't keep the hotel locked down for much longer. There had been complaints from the solicitors of several influential guests, including the brother of the chief constable, threatening action if their clients weren't released. The alleged suicide attempt of one of the mentally fragile guests hadn't helped her cause, since the press was linking it to her enforced incarceration of those who had come to the spa for spiritual healing.

She summoned DS Bristow. 'Larry, what are we getting by way of witness statements confirming Dawes's guilt?'

He shook his head. 'Diddly squat, boss. No one reported seeing him behaving suspiciously. The few guests and staff who had any contact with him described him as a really nice bloke, quiet and polite.'

'Damn! What have we got from Digital Forensics about the stuff on his phone?'

'Apart from the pic of the gun, they couldn't find anything suspicious. His calls and messages were mostly to his wife and this bloke, Bugsy. His internet trawls were mainly about rugby scores.'

'Of course, he wouldn't be conducting OCG business on it. He'll have a burner phone for that. Have we searched his room?'

'Yep. We did it while his wife was with you, being interviewed for assault. Nothing of interest. Should we ask the local cops to get a warrant to search his house?'

Lorraine shook her head. 'No point. A police officer as deeply into corruption as Dawes will be "cuckooing". He'll have taken over some poor simple sod's address as a base for his activities. Probably a young woman that he's nicked for soliciting in the past and who's scared of him.'

'That might fit,' suggested Bristow. 'There were a couple of messages from someone called Carlene, asking if he was having a good time. Could be code for something else.'

Lorraine frowned. 'There's a lot about this character we don't know. He's ruthless. He could be covering himself in all sorts of ways — threats of violence, blackmail, extortion, protection rackets, who knows?'

'There's another possibility,' suggested DC Nosworthy. 'What's that, Noz?'

'He might be innocent.'

* * *

When the custody sergeant unlocked the door of his cell, Jack thought he was facing another long interrogation. DI Long was like a dog with a bone. She wouldn't accept any explanation for the circumstances other than that he was guilty and it was simply a matter of time before she proved it. Why didn't he do himself a favour and come clean? Then they could put him away for murder and corruption, along with all his accomplices, and get on with their lives.

'Mr Dawes, I need some information from you.' It was DC Nosworthy, without the boss. He nodded to the custody officer. 'It's all right, Nigel. You go and have your break.'

'You sure, Noz?' The officer had been on duty a number of hours and was keen to go to the canteen for his bacon roll and mug of tea.

'Positive. I can handle this bloke.'

The custody officer left and Noz sat down cautiously.

'I'm not violent, Detective Constable Nosworthy, just bloody fed up that nobody's listening to me,' said Jack. 'And when they do listen, they don't believe a word I say.'

'Please call me Noz, sir. I promised your wife I'd tell you that she came here, to try to speak to you.'

'Corrie was here? How did she manage that? I thought all the guests were told not to leave the hotel.'

'They were. Mrs Dawes employed . . . unorthodox methods. She assaulted a constable and got herself arrested.'

'Oh no, Corrie,' Jack groaned, his head in his hands. 'Where is she now?'

'She's back in the hotel. From what she has told me, two of her friends are staying in the hotel next door. They're planning to obtain evidence that proves you're innocent.'

'That'll be Cynthia and Carlene — the other two Cs. That's all I need.'

'Sorry?' Noz was baffled.

'Never mind, Noz. It's very good of you to tell me what's going on.'

'I wouldn't normally, sir. This might sound insubordinate, but I'm not comfortable with the way the DI and the DS are investigating your case. I joined the service, and CID in particular, to catch villains. I believe that first you gather the evidence, then you arrest the suspect, not the other way around. I think they've made their minds up without any real proof. Do you want me to give your wife a message?'

'Yes please, Noz. Tell her I love her and I know she means well, but she mustn't interfere. There are dangerous people behind this and she could get hurt. We have to leave it to the police. I'm confident they'll get there eventually. Thank you for your help, Noz, but don't get yourself into trouble on my behalf. You have a career to consider.'

After Noz had gone, Jack was deep in thought. He was touched that Corrie and her pals were doing some sleuthing of their own, but if DI Long found out, the Three Cs could well end up in the nick alongside him. Or worse, 'punished' by some underworld thugs for snooping into affairs they didn't understand.

CHAPTER FIFTEEN

DCS Garwood strode down the corridor and burst into the MIT room as if he expected to catch the team playing darts or listening to the cricket. They had been suspiciously quiet, although no murders had been reported for some time, so it was to be expected. He looked around. 'Where's Acting Detective Inspector Malone?'

'Sick leave, sir.'

'Toothache, sir.'

'He was in agony, sir.'

It was when Aled started to describe Bugsy's fictitious root canal filling, in gory detail, accompanied by drilling sound effects, that Garwood, who had a phobia of dentists, had had enough. 'All right, DC Williams, that'll do. Notify me when he's back, and in the meantime, if you need guidance from a senior officer, you know where to find me.'

Garwood was suspicious. First Cynthia had gone missing, allegedly to 'do his job for him', and now Malone. He feared a conspiracy was forming to get Dawes out of jail. If he did anything, it could be construed as collusion. Better to pretend he knew nothing about it. Cynthia could simply have gone to the spa to stay with her friend and have some female pampering nonsense. Nothing more. In fact, when he'd rung Cynthia's mobile, Corrie Dawes had answered it and told him his wife was having a massage. He'd said he hoped that she and Cynthia were enjoying the spa and rung off. As far as he'd been told, Malone was off sick with toothache. He decided a little more masterly inactivity was required.

* * *

'Phew, that was close,' said Mitch. 'What's the latest from the sarge?'

'He's booked into a hotel, next door to the Now to Zen,' answered Aled.

'Mrs Garwood's there, too. And Carlene, Mrs Dawes's deputy,' put in Gemma.

Clive looked up from his computer screen. 'Blimey, the storm clouds are gathering.'

'You've got to feel sorry for the poor buggers on the receiving end,' said Mitch. 'They won't know what's hit 'em.'

Clive tapped on his keyboard. 'I've managed to get into the Now to Zen check-in technology. It was fairly simple — their security is weak. Most guests prefer face-to-face service at the reception desk, with the exception of a few who used the self-service app, which lets you book directly. Those people use their individual booking number on arrival to check in through the hotel kiosk. No need to interact with reception staff at all.'

'Much quicker,' confirmed Gemma. 'But I expect they would have had to meet with a real person to book their treatment programmes, wouldn't they?'

'Not necessarily. It's what I'd expect from the Now to Zen Corporation,' said Clive. 'It's a revenue optimisation tool. It's a subtle way of upselling guests. Because they're able to book dinner reservations, spa treatments and any other sports activities online, guests are tempted towards the more exclusive options.'

'What's the relevance of this, Clive?' asked Aled.

'It means that chummy could have booked in and stayed there without the staff or management having any personal contact with him at all. He'd have booked his own pampering sessions and his meals, everything.'

'I'm assuming you didn't find any registrations in the name of Eddie Clayton,' Mitch asked, more in jest than expectation.

''Fraid not.'

'That system's a bit risky, isn't it?' Gemma asked. 'They could have any number of dodgy characters staying there, and they wouldn't know. Surely they have to prove ID?'

'There's no law concerning proof of ID in hotels in England. Not that it would bother OCG members if there were. They have multiple IDs in several names, both passports and credit cards — all forgeries.'

'So the bottom line is that our man is staying there, with or without the stolen money, and nobody has a clue who he is.'

'With the boss, the sarge, Mrs Dawes, Mrs Garwood and Carlene down there, there's bound to be some kind of activity soon,' said Aled.

And there was, but not quite what they expected.

* * *

'Sergeant Bugsy, it's *soooo* good to see you!' Carlene threw her arms around him. Bugsy had been something of an uncle to Carlene since Corrie had taken her on at Coriander's Cuisine, some years ago.

'Sergeant Malone, *I'm* glad you're here, too,' Cynthia added. 'Frankly, we're not making much progress on our own.'

'I'd be obliged if you didn't mention it to the DCS, Mrs Garwood. He thinks I'm off sick with toothache.'

'Well, I left him a note to say I'd gone to catch a killer, so he can make of that what he pleases. What's our next move, Sergeant?'

'How is Mrs Dawes holding up?' he asked.

'I'll ring her on video and you can talk to her.' Carlene hit the speed dial and soon, Bugsy was face to face with Corrie.

'Hello, Bugsy! Where did you spring from? Jack will be so grateful that you've come to help. My sports buddy, Louis, did what you suggested. He shouted in all the restaurants at breakfast time, when most people were together, and in all the lounges and corridors. Obviously, our man didn't jump up and identify himself.'

'But he knows that someone's onto him, knows his real name, and suspects that he killed Della,' confirmed Bugsy. 'That'll force him into some sort of action. He isn't safe there anymore.'

'Well, he can't just check out,' reasoned Corrie. 'None of us can. The SIO investigating the murder is keeping everyone locked down here, until she has enough evidence to charge Jack. But my friend, Noz, told me that she's being leaned on by solicitors, demanding she let people go.'

'Who's Noz?'

'Detective Constable Jeff Nosworthy of Brightsea CID. He's been helping me get messages to Jack, at considerable risk to himself, I might add.'

'Good man.' At least one copper in Brightsea was thinking straight.

'There are some rather important businesspeople here, who came for a short break to chill out from the stress of running their consortia. They didn't anticipate being here for this long. They're threatening her with all sorts of legal penalties and saying they'll sue for lost revenue. According to Noz, she's having to let people go, but they have to provide ID, DNA and fingerprints first. It's kind of contrary to PACE guidance, Noz says, but she's justifying it by saying if they don't consent, that makes them suspects.'

'Eddie Clayton won't risk that. He daren't. He knows that as soon as they get his prints and match them to the PNC, he'll be nicked. Now, he's only got one choice — he'll run for it, under the noses of the police. My NCA mate, Charlie, says he's wriggled out of tighter scrapes in the past.'

Corrie was apprehensive. 'I doubt if DI Long will even be interested. She's only concerned with charging Jack and getting him put away.'

'That isn't going to happen,' said Bugsy, firmly. 'Trust me.'

* * *

When Eddie Clayton heard his name called by that flashy sports coach, he knew it was a fishing trip and they were getting close. Much too close. He should have made a dash for it, as soon as he'd seen the end of Della, but he'd timed it badly. He thought he'd have longer, but that smart-arse copper and his wife had found her body at stupid o'clock at night. Then, all hell had broken loose, the place was crawling with police wherever you went, and he hadn't had an opportunity to disappear, as he'd planned. He carried forged documents, which would confirm his assumed identity, but fingerprints didn't lie.

He had only one option left. He'd have to make a break for it, and he'd already worked out how. He just needed the assistance of a charming but gullible lady, and he knew the very one. Then he'd pick up the money and be on the next plane to Saudi.

* * *

In the honeymoon suite, Antonio Di Vincenzo had been thinking along very similar lines to Eddie. His new wife, Abbie, was being tiresome.

'Honey, why don't we just show the cops our passports, give them our fingerprints and then we can be on the plane to Monaco?'

Toni could not envisage a worse scenario. 'No, *mia bella*, we should wait for your *papà* to send his lawyers. They will get us out without all that. It's a violation of our privacy and human rights. I do not think we should be queueing up with all the commonplace people in this hotel. We should not have to do it.'

Abbie was continually impressed by her husband's English. The son of an Italian count, brought up in Sicily, his vocabulary was better than hers, even with her Ivy League education. He was so adorable, she could eat him. 'OK, sweetheart. Whatever you say. I guess I'll go get my nails done.'

* * *

In the hotel next door, Bugsy was considering his next move. No point in him coming here to help, if he wasn't going to do something. After all, he wasn't on holiday. He was working. The only way to convince this DI Long that Jack was neither corrupt nor a murderer was to present her with Eddie Clayton. With this in mind, Bugsy decided a bit of 'obbo' was called for.

It had been some time since his police observation days. DC Mitchell was the expert. He could blend in with his surroundings and rarely lost a target. All the same, Bugsy was pretty certain that having been rattled, Eddie would be bailing out anytime soon, and it was his job to grab him.

He'd got an idea of the layout of the Now to Zen from Corrie. She was highly observant and could describe all the ways in and out. She also knew how many uniforms had been deployed to secure them. With this knowledge, Bugsy reckoned that Eddie's best escape route would be through the kitchens and out the back door. There was only one copper guarding it — most were at the front, sides and exits leading to the various outdoor facilities such as tennis courts, terraces and the like.

He found himself a spot where he could watch who came and went and settled down to wait. He'd stashed enough food in a backpack to last for at least several hours, but he reckoned Eddie wouldn't hang about, now that he knew his number was up.

CHAPTER SIXTEEN

David opened his eyes. He tried to move, but everything hurt. He was bandaged and strapped up, attached to a drip, and wired to a bedside cardiac monitor. For a time, he couldn't remember what had happened to him. Then, gradually, it started to filter back. Slowly at first, then in glorious technicolour. He remembered the pier, lit up like Las Vegas. He'd been up high somewhere, leaning forward, the better to see it. Then he'd lost his balance. He could remember the air rushing past until — nothing. There had been someone up there with him. Who was it? Then it came to him and he muttered her name.

'Meredith.'

The police officer sitting by his bed had been instructed to call for assistance as soon as he showed signs of regaining consciousness. She spoke to him. 'It's all right, David. You just rest. I'm going to fetch the nurse.' She hurried out.

Moments later, a figure emerged from the crowded seating area, outside in the corridor. She looked around her, then slipped swiftly in. She knew she had little time before the police officer and a doctor would come, so she had to do it quickly. She pulled a pillow from beneath his head and without a moment's hesitation, she pushed it down over his face. He was too weak to struggle and, for the second time, he believed his life was at an end.

Just seconds later, another figure followed her in.

Rainbow was horrified at what she saw. 'Meredith! What on earth are you doing?'

Rainbow had given her DNA and fingerprints, like Meredith, in order to get out of the Now to Zen to visit David. She had taken his attempted suicide badly, believing she could have helped him. Now she couldn't believe what she was seeing. She wrested the pillow from Meredith and grappled with her, screaming for help, until the doctor and police officer burst in.

'What's going on?' demanded the doctor. 'I won't have brawling on my ward. This man's seriously ill. Whatever you're fighting about, take it outside!'

Rainbow was desperate. 'No, you don't understand. Meredith was trying to smother David with this pillow.' She appealed to the policewoman. 'Arrest her! Quick!'

Now that David was conscious and would soon be able to speak, Meredith realized that he'd tell them what she'd done. The game was up. She had to get away. She glared around her like a cornered rat, then made a dash for the door, throwing Rainbow to the ground and elbowing the doctor out of the way.

But the police officer was too quick for her. She put out a foot and tripped her, then slapped on the handcuffs, while she lay on the floor. Meredith screeched like a wild cat, spitting and screaming all the imprecations she could, before she was jostled out of the room. The police officer called for backup. She didn't know why this girl had been trying to kill the man she was there to guard, but she wasn't about to let her go.

The shocked doctor examined David and the devices monitoring his vital signs. Surprisingly, he found him none the worse, despite his second ordeal. He turned to Rainbow. 'I think you should leave.'

David became agitated and tried to speak but couldn't find the strength. He tried to reach out his hand, but it was tethered to a drip.

'Do you want this other young woman to stay?' the doctor asked.

David nodded and tried to smile at Rainbow. His sight was somewhat impaired by the bandages around his head, but he could still make out her perfect heart-shaped face and the shining hair falling around her shoulders in auburn curls.

'Just for a few minutes,' agreed the doctor against his better judgement. His ward, it seemed, had gone mad. 'He needs rest.' He went outside to see if the police reinforcements had arrived. The hospital was a private one and David's treatment was being funded by the Carter Jefferson Corporation. It wouldn't look good if something happened to this patient while under his care. Visitors were supposed to be carefully monitored. He wanted answers about who had let in a murderous psychopath.

Rainbow sat down beside David's bed and took his free hand. 'I'm so sorry. This is awful. Why did Meredith attack you like that? She must have gone mad. She's always been a bit different to the rest of us — streaks of harsh orange in her aura, indicating excess, addiction and obsession — but I didn't have her down as unhinged.'

David knew exactly why. For the same reason she had tried to persuade him that it was Penny Hawkins who was stealing money from the company. All that nonsense about her online gambling and huge debts. He was pretty sure he'd discover it was Meredith who was the gambling addict with a massive hole in her bank account.

'When you're better, we'll do another aura reading. You can tell me why you jumped off the roof and—'

David shook his head with great difficulty. He couldn't let Rainbow go on believing that. 'Didn't jump. Meredith pushed me.'

'Oh my goodness! Why does she want you dead?'

He took a deep, wincing breath. 'Money. Found out she's stealing.'

'No wonder she tried to suffocate you. Well, the police have got her now and happily, you're still alive to tell them what happened. I'm so glad I shall still be able to see you. That's if you want me to.' She took his hand and he realized he was very glad, too.

* * *

After the assault and Rainbow's statement of what she'd witnessed, they ran Meredith's prints through the police PNC, to check for a criminal record. They found plenty. She had form for fraud, embezzlement and all kinds of computer scams. Her gambling had escalated to the extent that it was on her record. Now she had two attempted murders to add to it.

Dick Hawkins was shocked. 'Didn't we check her background and references when she applied for the job?' he asked Penny.

'No. I always intended to have her vetted, but she was so good at the computer work, I just let her get on with it.' Penny made a mental note never to make that mistake again.

'At least now we know where the money was going. She'd been systematically syphoning cash from this and other Now to Zen spas for ages.'

'Will they close us down, do you think?'

'Probably,' said Dick. 'What with that, and all the other disasters that have been happening here, I'd be surprised if they didn't. Old Carter Jefferson III didn't make his billions by supporting failing businesses.'

* * *

Sir Marcus Wellbeloved smoothed the lapels of his Savile Row suit and straightened his silk tie. His Louis Vuitton suitcase was packed and waiting. When Dorothy Buncombe came out of her room in a tennis dress, ready for her lesson with Louis, he intercepted her.

'Good morning, Dorothy. May I say that you're looking exceptionally attractive, today.'

She blushed. 'Well, thank you, Sir Marcus. You're looking very smart yourself.' She noticed he had shaved off his beard and moustache, revealing a long scar down his cheek. She thought it looked dashing — like a duelling scar.

'I wonder if you would do me a favour, dear lady. I need your assistance with a small deception.'

Dorothy thought that sounded intriguing. 'Of course. I'll help if I can.'

He drew her to one side and lowered his voice. 'The thing is, I'm not in the import–export business. I work for MI6, the Secret Intelligence Service.'

She quivered. 'How exciting!'

'It's my job to disrupt the activity of hostile states, and at the moment, I'm attempting to keep one step ahead of an adversary — a rather dangerous spy.'

'And you need my help with that?' Dorothy almost swooned. *At last, a real-life James Bond.*

'I need to get out of here, but I can't afford to give the police my fingerprints. My identity is top secret. You do understand?'

'Oh, absolutely. What can I do?'

'I'm planning to make my escape through the kitchens and out of the back door. There's only one police officer on duty there. I hoped you could use your undoubted charm and allure to distract him while I slip out. Do you think you could do that?'

'I'm sure I could, Sir Marcus.'

'I'll stay out of sight, in the vegetable preparation area, until you have him in your thrall, then I'll steal past.'

'Right. Is there anything you need me to do after you've gone? Contact M — I mean, Head of Missions — and let them know?'

117

'No, nothing, thank you. I'll be forever in your debt, as will our country.' He slipped into the shadows behind a pallet of root vegetables.

How would Pussy Galore or Honey Ryder tackle this important assignment? Dorothy wondered. *They would use all their feminine wiles, of course.* She eased the neckline of her tennis dress a little lower and hitched up her skirt, affording a tantalizing glimpse of her matching knickers. She opened the back door and when she was level with the police officer, she pretended to trip on the step.

'Oww! Oww!' she yelped, prettily.

The copper immediately came to her aid. 'Are you hurt, madam?'

'Yes, I believe I've sprained my ankle. It's really painful.'

'Well, you won't be able to play tennis, now, will you? I think we'd better get you back inside so one of the physios can look at it.'

'Oh yes, please,' Dorothy simpered. 'Thank you so much. You're very kind.' She leaned heavily on him as he half-carried her to the lift, never once asking why she was attempting to access the tennis courts via the kitchen. Out of the corner of her eye, she saw Sir Marcus blow her a kiss and her heart leaped. He had several minutes to pick up his case and saunter out.

Once outside, he breathed a sigh of relief and made tracks towards the promenade, to pick up a taxi to the airport. He'd had to leave his car behind, but no matter. He'd buy another, smarter one, when he got to Saudi.

* * *

From his vantage point behind the perimeter hedge, Bugsy spotted him and congratulated himself on having correctly anticipated Eddie's movements. This bloke didn't have a beard, but it had to be him. All he needed to do now was arrest him, take him back to the station and question him until he confessed to the murder. Then Jack would be in the clear. He started to run after him but didn't call out, so as not to give him too much warning. He had a hunch that Clayton could probably outrun him, even carrying a suitcase. But before he could catch up, a big, black saloon pulled up alongside Eddie, and two heavies in suits and dark glasses lumbered out.

'Hello, Eddie. Remember us? The boss wants a word. Get in the car.'

Della, the bitch! She'd told them where he was. Eddie looked desperately around for a way out, but they had grabbed both his arms in an iron grip. They flung his suitcase in the back of the car and were about to shove him in after it, when Bugsy ran at them, shouting.

'Stop! I'm a police officer. Let that man go! He's under arrest.'

They were clearly unimpressed by this, as one of the thugs drew back a massive fist and Bugsy, sprinting at top speed and out of control, virtually ran onto it. He dropped where he stood. The thug put his boot into Bugsy's ribs several times for good measure. When he came round, he was lying in the gutter, spitting blood from two loose front teeth, with a growing crowd of concerned bystanders. His first thought was that now he wouldn't have to tell Garwood he'd lied. He really did need a dentist. His second thought was that the OCG had got Clayton. He was as good as dead.

CHAPTER SEVENTEEN

'Honestly, Sergeant Bugsy,' Carlene scolded. 'And you told *me* not to do anything dangerous.' He was sitting in her room while she ministered to his smashed face. She suspected he could even have broken ribs. 'From now on, it's going to be a diet of soup for you.'

'I know. And I wouldn't mind about me ribs and teeth, but I lost the bugger! I'll never live it down when the team finds out — especially Mitch, the "obbo" king.'

'Never mind that,' said Cynthia. 'If they're the gang running the racket, they could have killed you.'

'They probably would have, but I guess they were in a bit of a hurry and didn't want to waste time on a portly copper, who was trying to arrest their man. They'd have been told to get him back to the boss as quickly as possible, so they could find out where he'd put the money. We're most likely talking hundreds of thousands, even for an average drugs deal. Minus what he's already spent, of course.'

Carlene mopped the blood from his chin. 'I don't suppose you were able to get the registration number?'

'As it happens, I did. I doubt it will get us any further forward, though. These blokes nick your car, do the job then set fire to it, before you even know it's been stolen. It's how they operate.'

'I say, what a frightful bunch of rotten eggs,' declaimed Cynthia, defaulting to 'spiffing' mode.

'Sorry, Mrs Garwood. What's a rotten egg?' asked Bugsy.

'It's someone who's thoroughly, intrinsically inclined to behave badly and cause trouble. Or, in the vernacular of the underworld, a shit-faced arsehole!' cursed Cynthia.

Bugsy wondered if her old man knew she used language like that.

* * *

Later, Bugsy emailed Clive to do an ANPR check and it was as he suspected. The car had been stolen from outside the home of a high court judge, then found burned out on a piece of waste ground.

'He must have used distraction tactics to get out of that hotel unnoticed,' mused Bugsy. 'One minute there was a copper outside, then he seemed to be talking to someone from inside the kitchen. I couldn't see who. A few minutes later, chummy comes waltzing out, calm as you like, and walks away through the gates.'

'We'll ask Mrs D if she knows who helped him,' suggested Carlene. She reached for her phone.

The result was inconclusive. Corrie reported that many people were leaving, legitimately, having given their finger-prints and DNA and been cleared.

'I'm not suggesting that all the guests who are left here are criminals, reluctant to be identified. They've booked in for a holiday and intend to enjoy all the facilities. As for me, DI Long has intimated — and by that, I mean ordered — that I should stay here, until she's dealt with Jack to her satisfaction. She won't be happy until she's had him hung, drawn and quartered.'

'Mrs Dawes, I watched Eddie Clayton walk away,' said Bugsy. 'Minutes later, he was bundled into a car by some

OCG characters. My guess is, he won't last much longer, once he's told them where he put the money he nicked. Can you do a bit of sleuthing? Find out who helped him to leg it? We need to convince the law that he killed Della before he ends up in tins of dogfood, which will make it very much more difficult.'

Corrie was resolute. 'I'm on it.' Even on video call, she could see that someone had tried to rearrange his features. 'Are you all right, Bugsy?'

'Yeah, fine. I might find it a bit awkward biting into a bacon roll for a couple of days, but Chef Carlene here says she'll make it into a soup sandwich for me.'

* * *

As it turned out, finding out who had helped Clayton escape was easier than Corrie had first thought. Dorothy was still basking in the afterglow of having helped an MI6 agent to carry out an important mission. She told Peggy, who harrumphed her disapproval and told her she was a fool.

'If he's a special agent, what was he doing in Brightsea? Ask yourself that!' She was pulling on her riding gear, ready for an invigorating gallop on the Downs. She had to admit, despite her initial misgivings, that her back had improved considerably after a programme of physio massages.

'He was after a dangerous spy. His job is to disrupt the activities of hostile states, and I helped him.' She sighed. 'I may change my name to Vesper or Solitaire.'

Peggy sniffed. 'Did he ask you for money?'

'No, of course he didn't. Why would he do that?'

'Because he's a con artist, preying on silly women like you. I bet his name isn't Marcus Wellbeloved, either. No wonder he didn't want them to take his fingerprints. He's probably wanted by every police force in the country. I don't know about changing your name — I reckon Dotty suits you perfectly.' She strode out, leaving Dorothy wondering if she might be right.

Later, she met Corrie in the lounge. It was common knowledge that Corrie was the wife of the police officer in custody on suspicion of murdering the woman in the whirlpool, although nobody believed it. She must know something about criminals and how they operated. Dorothy decided to run the spy story past her, to see what she thought. What harm could it do?

Corrie listened carefully to Dorothy's disclosure about Sir Marcus actually being an undercover MI6 agent. Her reaction was as explosive as it was unexpected. 'It was him all along!' she exclaimed. 'Sir Marcus Wellbeloved was Eddie Clayton! I should have guessed.' Now she needed to establish that 'Sir Marcus' was already present in the hotel when Della was murdered. She rushed off, leaving Dorothy bemused and wondering what she meant.

* * *

Corrie hurried to reception, now manned by a new girl. 'Hello—' Corrie peered at the name on her lanyard — 'Phoebe. I'm sorry to bother you, but please can you look on the computer and tell me when Sir Marcus Wellbeloved first checked in?'

Phoebe was doubtful. Her real job was a nail technician, specializing in acrylic extensions. She didn't know the protocols relating to giving one guest information about another. But it didn't seem particularly personal, so she tapped a few keys and came up with the date. It was a week prior to when Corrie and Jack had arrived, so a week before they had found the body of Della Clayton.

Corrie pulled out Cynthia's borrowed phone and fingered a contact. 'Bugsy? Eddie Clayton has been posing as Sir Marcus Wellbeloved. The receptionist says he checked himself in online some days before Della Clayton was found dead.'

'Marcus Wellbeloved? Blimey! I wonder where that moniker came from. You couldn't make it up, could you?'

'Actually, you could, and he did,' observed Corrie. 'He needed the kind of name that would give the impression he was respectable and wealthy.'

'I doubt if it was his idea to book into a fancy spa hotel, though,' said Bugsy. 'I reckon Della told him to meet her there, otherwise she'd grass. She wanted her share of the money. He went there and killed her to shut her up, but you and Jack found the body sooner than he planned. Next thing he knew, the place was full of cops, and he couldn't just pack his bag and walk out.'

Corrie frowned. 'Hmm. But that doesn't explain why she chose to meet in a Now to Zen hotel. Why go to all the bother of getting a fake uniform and sneaking in past the doorman? She could simply have arranged a meeting in a pub or a café, probably in one of the downmarket quarters of London.'

'Good point,' conceded Bugsy. 'She must have had some other reason for wanting to be there. Now she's dead, we'll probably never find out.'

* * *

'Sir Marcus, how lovely to see you.' The city bank manager recognized him immediately. He kept a safety deposit box there, which he accessed quite frequently. She wondered what was in it. Probably important papers — stocks, bonds and property deeds. She doubted it would be cash. Customers were discouraged from keeping cash in their box, because it wasn't protected by insurance.

She was proud that her bank had a modern approach to deposit boxes. Each one was protected by four levels of security — key card, PIN, the latest fingerprint technology and a key. A customer needed all four to gain access. Sir Marcus didn't need to venture into the vault to retrieve his valuables, which had once been the case. She directed him to a private viewing room, where his box would be robotically delivered. He knew the routine and put his key card in the slot to open the door.

She was surprised that he appeared to have brought two bodyguards, who stuck closely to him as he entered the room. In addition, one of his hands was heavily bandaged with grubby, bloodstained rags.

'Sir Marcus, you've injured your hand. Can you manage? You'll need to provide a fingerprint.'

'Yes, I'm fine. It's the other hand I need.'

She still sensed something was wrong. 'Will these two gentlemen be accompanying you?' she asked.

'Yes, love. We'll be going in with him, all right.' The man laughed unpleasantly. He was carrying a large holdall.

A short while later, the three men emerged, one of them carrying the holdall, which looked considerably heavier. The manager thought Sir Marcus looked far from well. 'Can I get you something, Sir Marcus? A glass of water? A cup of coffee?'

'He hasn't got time, love,' said one of the thugs. 'He's got another appointment.' He leered at her. They left, almost carrying Sir Marcus between them.

* * *

They found Eddie 'Coke' Clayton's body in a skip the following day. All his fingers had been cut off and both his legs were broken. Finally, someone had put a bullet in the back of his head. He was identified by his DNA on the PNC criminal record check and the news reached the NCA almost instantly.

Charlie phoned Bugsy. 'The bastards got him, Bugsy — and the cash.'

'I know. I got two loose front teeth, a redesigned nose and a couple of busted ribs trying to stop 'em. It's a bugger. If I hadn't been unconscious, I might have been able to put out a call for a pursuit car.'

'Not your fault, mate. You weren't to know they were lying in wait for him.'

I suppose they "persuaded" him to tell them where he'd put the money.'

'You bet they did.' Charlie explained the injuries Eddie had sustained before they shot him.

'Nasty. Why didn't he tell them before it got that vicious?'

'He did. The bank manager was the last person to see him, other than the OCG. She says that when he fetched up with two goons to get the cash, only his left hand was injured. He needed the right one for a thumbprint.'

'So what was all the other barbaric treatment for?'

'Usually, when one gangster kills another, they dispose of the body in a way that we never find it. But in this case, they left it in open sight, in a skip, as a warning to anybody else who felt like double-crossing them. It was a gangland execution of the worst kind.'

'You know, Charlie, I don't envy you your job. It's gruesome enough in the MIT sometimes, but at least I can eat me dinner when I get home at night.'

'Yeah, and it's worse when you've lost the target, his wife and the money. And we're no nearer to cracking the OCG. If only we could find someone who'd seen some of the gang, especially the head of the organization, and lived to tell the tale. Someone who could identify them and any place they'd been stashing the stuff, so we could harvest some DNA and prints. I'm sure we could match them to our records and pick 'em up. Trouble is, anyone who's been that close ends up dead before we can reach them.'

CHAPTER EIGHTEEN

DI Long had been informed by her chief superintendent — who'd had his ear chewed off by a high-ranking officer in the NCA — that the handling of Della Clayton's murder was the subject of an ongoing internal inquiry. The Independent Office for Police Conduct had been tasked with determining what had gone wrong.

Lorraine was furious. 'And as the poor, bloody SIO, I suppose that means I get all the blame,' she raged to Bristow.

The inquiry had decided that in all probability, Eddie Clayton, aka Sir Marcus Wellbeloved — a known felon — had killed his wife, Della Clayton. The motive was to prevent her from disclosing his whereabouts to the organized crime group of which he had been an active member, until he had absconded with the proceeds of a drug deal. He had since been executed by said OCG.

'Well, three cheers for Captain Hindsight!' Lorraine slammed down her coffee mug.

The report continued, somewhat acrimoniously, that not only had the NCA lost a vital lead to smashing the organization — a case that they had been working on for some time — but they'd also lost the money from the drugs operation. All they had achieved was taking the Taurus 856 out of circulation.

The chief superintendent told DI Long, in no uncertain terms, that her investigation was closed and the man she had been holding in custody, Detective Inspector Jack Dawes, was to be released, immediately, without charge. And she'd better hope he wasn't the type to bear a grudge.

Lorraine was outraged. The real killer had been swanning around the Now to Zen under her very nose, masquerading as a member of the blasted aristocracy. Meanwhile, she had been wasting time with a copper who was no more corrupt than she was. Everything he'd told her had turned out to be the truth. Never mind promotion, she'd be lucky to come out of this with a traffic job.

'I don't believe it, Larry. I was positive the Dawes man was guilty. He fitted all the stereotypes of a police officer who'd crossed the line — gone over to the dark side.' She looked across at DC Nosworthy. 'Why are you pulling that face, Noz?'

'Because I don't think he did, boss. All the evidence was circumstantial. I believe he'd have caught Clayton for us, if we'd given him half a chance. It was his wife, Corrie, who eventually flushed him out, but we didn't listen to her, did we? If we'd been outside, mob-handed, waiting for him to make a break for it, we might have grabbed him before the gang did. As it was, Sergeant Malone got a smack in the mouth and broken ribs for his trouble and chummy's dead. And we're still no closer to finding the money, the drugs or the man at the top who's directing the whole set-up.'

'Oh, really? Well, aren't you the smart-arse? Did you think Dawes was innocent, Larry?'

'No, boss. I think he's a smarmy git and he'll be laughing up his sleeve now. Let's just hope he doesn't do us for wrongful arrest.'

Lorraine sighed. 'Thank goodness I didn't charge him.'

* * *

Jack certainly wasn't laughing up his sleeve or anywhere else, for that matter. When DC Nosworthy came to tell him he was to be released, he could have hugged him. The custody sergeant gave him back his possessions and shook his hand, and Noz escorted him out.

'You'll be happy to get back to Mrs Dawes, sir. She's been working so hard to get you out of here. So have her friends. And Sergeant Malone is here, too.'

Jack beamed. 'Bugsy's here?'

'Yes, sir.'

'Good man. I'll have to treat him to a slap-up Now to Zen dinner.'

'That might be tricky, sir. He's having a few problems chewing at the moment.'

'Why?'

'Eddie Clayton's "friends" took exception to Sergeant Malone trying to arrest him.'

Jack frowned. 'You mean Bugsy was beaten up?'

'In a manner of speaking. The strategy worked perfectly — there just weren't enough coppers to carry it through.'

'Thanks for letting me know, Noz. I'll get back to the hotel. I need to make sure Bugsy's OK, and I could do with a good meal, myself.'

'There's a car waiting for you outside, sir.'

* * *

Noz had called ahead and Corrie was waiting for Jack, as were Cynthia, Carlene and Bugsy. Most of the staff and guests who hadn't yet left the Now to Zen also turned out to welcome him.

'We never believed you were guilty, Jack.' Dorothy kissed him on the cheek. 'That Sir Marcus was obviously a criminal. He didn't fool me one bit.'

'Hypocrite!' Peggy hissed at her, but she was pleased to see justice had prevailed. 'I couldn't stand that po-faced detective inspector. Put her on a decent mount and set her off across the gallops — that'll soon knock the arrogance out of her!'

'Hello, Jack. I'm Kelly-Anne, your spa buddy. I'm very glad you're back.'

Jack laughed. 'Thank you, Kelly-Anne. But if you've come to offer me a relaxing dip in a twilight whirlpool, I'll pass, if it's OK with you.'

Fred Withenshaw shook his hand vigorously. 'Eh, lad, I'm reet glad to see yer. That policewoman's a nasty piece of work. She knows nowt about folk.'

Rita nodded her agreement. 'What was she thinking, locking up a decent fellow in a prison cell? You can't trust anybody these days.'

Louis clapped Jack on the back with such force that he nearly fell over. 'Hey, dude. If you want a workout after sitting around in a cell, just say the word. I'm your man.'

Rainbow drifted into his orbit, her flowing skirts wafting around her, like a tent that had escaped from its moorings in a gale. 'You'll be pleased to learn, Mr Dawes, that your aura is now green, the colour of peace, healing and harmony.' She gave him an ethereal smile and floated away.

Dick and Penny Hawkins were mortified at what had happened. Dick had every suspicion that they would soon be looking down the wrong end of a lawsuit from at least one guest. 'Please feel free to spend the rest of your holiday at the expense of the Now to Zen Corporation.'

'Thank you,' said Jack, when all he really wanted to do was go home. But he knew Corrie would want to stay — and there was still something niggling away at the back of his mind.

* * *

That evening, Jack and Corrie invited Bugsy, Cynthia and Carlene for dinner. It was a relaxed meal in the Cheerful Chophouse — Jack's choice. There was a lot of laughter and general relief that DI Long had finally been forced to slacken her moray eel jaws and release her prey.

'Now that's all over, perhaps we can go back to work and leave you guys to chill.' Carlene was cutting Bugsy's steak into bite-sized pieces.

'I keep getting missed calls on your phone from George,' grinned Corrie. 'I think you'd better speak to him, Cyn, before he comes down here to see what you're up to.'

'Let him stew a bit longer,' Cynthia declared, taking back her phone. 'It'll serve him right for not pulling any strings, like I asked him.'

'It wasn't so much that he wouldn't pull any strings,' complained Bugsy. 'He threatened to slap Reg 15 notices on us if we did anything to help the guvnor. Needless to say, we all ignored it and got stuck in. The team are over the moon you've been cleared, Jack. They can't wait to have you back.'

'Thanks. I can't tell you how grateful I am. And if the chief super tries to take action against anybody, I'll threaten to resign.'

'He won't,' Cynthia assured him. 'I'll see to that.'

Jack was forking his way through a large helping of corned beef hash. It was exactly the same meal that he'd had in the Grosvenor Room, except for the description on the Cheerful Chophouse menu: *corned beef hash with baked beans and brown sauce (optional)*. 'One thing I've learned from this experience,' he said, 'is that I'd rather be a cop than a crook. I realize that being arrested is an occupational hazard for career criminals, but for everyone else, it's bloody terrifying!'

* * *

Back in their room, Corrie opened the bottle of champagne that had been left for them, compliments of the hotel. 'This is nice, isn't it, sweetheart? I just fancy some fizz.' She handed Jack a glass. 'Wasn't it lovely that everyone came down to welcome you back?'

'Yes, it was. Did I see a new girl on the desk?'

Corrie frowned. 'Of course, you won't know about that. Do you remember David? He was the quiet lad, spent most of his time in his room, on his computer.'

'Vaguely. I only saw him a couple of times.'

'Turns out he's a senior software engineer, employed by Jefferson. He was here to find out who'd planted a malicious code and was syphoning cash from the corporation. It was Meredith.'

'That's a surprise. I'm guessing she's been sacked?'

'Worse than that. She found out what he was doing from his internet activity, lured him up to the rooftop swimming pool and pushed him off.'

'Bloody hell! Poor bloke.'

'He wasn't killed. He landed on some rubbish sacks.'

'Thank goodness. So was that the end of it?'

'Not quite. She went to the hospital and tried to suffocate him with a pillow. Rainbow stopped her.' She sighed. 'I think they'll make a colourful couple, once he explains auraology to his mother.'

Jack nearly choked on his champagne. 'How did you describe this place? A spiritual paradise of relaxation and pampering? So far, it's been more like a harrowing episode from some particularly ghastly soap opera.'

Corrie patted his shoulder. 'Well, it's all over now, darling. We can spend the rest of the holiday doing what we set out to do — transforming our minds and bodies into a state of Zen.'

Jack didn't reply.

'That *is* what we'll do, isn't it, Jack?'

'Yes, of course, sweetheart. I just need to have a chat with Bugsy before he leaves.'

'Why?' Corrie was growing evermore suspicious.

'Something on my mind. A few things that don't quite add up. Bugsy's a great sounding board. He'll tell me if I'm right.'

'Jack — no! Please say you aren't going to do any more detecting.'

Jack topped up her glass. 'No, nothing like that, my little food processor. Just satisfying my policeman's curiosity.'

* * *

Jack wasn't the only one keen to have a chat with Bugsy. Miriam Bennett had heard from her facial exfoliation aesthetician, who'd heard it from Kelly-Anne, who'd been told by Dorothy Buncombe's security guard, that Sir Marcus — who wasn't really Sir Marcus, but a mobster called Eddie — had been kidnapped by a couple of thugs waiting for him outside the hotel. They'd bundled him into a car. Police had found his mutilated body in a skip.

Loud bells began to ring. The kidnap story was identical to the one Tim had told her as his excuse for abandoning her. She hadn't believed a word of it, of course. Well, who would have? Especially given Tim's track record for fibbing. But what if he'd been telling the truth for once? Apparently, a Detective Sergeant Malone had tried to prevent Sir Marcus's kidnap and had been beaten up in the attempt.

She tracked him down and told him her concerns. 'I'm sorry now that I didn't pay more attention to what Tim said. What do you think, Sergeant?'

Bugsy was immediately alert. If Timothy Bennett's story was true, he may be able to supply the NCA with some valuable information. What was it Charlie had said about finding someone who'd seen some of the gang, especially the boss, and lived to tell the tale? Someone who could identify them and where they'd been stashing the stuff?

'Can we phone your husband, Mrs Bennett?'

'No, I'm afraid not. I've got his mobile phone and we don't have a landline. I don't even know if he's at home now. I phoned the used-car dealership where he works and the Nag's Head, where he spends the rest of his time, but he isn't there, either.'

'Have you been home to look for him?'

'No.' She looked contrite. 'I wasn't very kind to him, you see. I was certain he'd made up that preposterous story to fob me off, and I was angry that he'd think I was stupid enough to believe it. It wasn't until I heard that the same thing had happened to the man calling himself Sir Marcus, who did bear a slight resemblance to Tim, that I realized he'd been telling the truth. They would have killed him, if he hadn't escaped.'

They might still try, thought Bugsy. 'Can you remember exactly what Tim told you?'

She tried to think back — it seemed a long time ago, even though it wasn't. 'He left the hotel during dinner, intending to go to a nightclub on the promenade. He'd only gone a short way when he was forced into a car by a couple of thugs. They took him to a warehouse and they were going to cut off his fingers, one at a time, until he told them where the money was — of course, he didn't know anything about any money. When the boss of the gang arrived, he must have realized Tim wasn't who they wanted, but now they had to kill him, because he'd seen them. Before they could do it, a rival gang turned up and there was a fight. Tim got away in the confusion. He said the man they were really after was still in the hotel and he was dangerous. That would be Sir Marcus, who had a beard and moustache very like Tim's, hence the mistake, and now he's been murdered. Do you think Tim's in any danger, Sergeant Malone?'

'I'm not sure but I think we should have him picked up, just in case. The National Crime Agency will want to speak to him. He has some useful information that might help them smash a dangerous organized crime gang. I'll put out a MISPER — a missing person's report. We'll soon find him. Thank you for speaking to me, Mrs Bennett, and try not to worry.'

CHAPTER NINETEEN

'Tonino, honey, I'm bored.' Abbie had had enough of the Brightsea Now to Zen, with all the disruption and mayhem the murder had caused, never mind the guy who had fallen off the roof. Her fascination with the 'Englishness' of the coast was rapidly wearing off. It didn't seem romantic any longer. 'Can't we go to Monaco, now?'

'We'll go as soon as your father's lawyers arrive. Their plane has been delayed by storms.'

She put her arms around his neck and wheedled, 'I don't get why we can't just leave, babe. The cops don't want ID and prints anymore — they got the guy who killed that poor woman. In any case, everyone knows who we are. Our wedding photos were in all the top celebrity magazines, here and in the States.'

Antonio snapped. He pulled free from her arms in a temper. 'Well, I say we can't — and that's an end of it!'

Abbie was shocked into silence. Antonio had never spoken to her like that before. She picked up her handbag and stormed out. Her mother, Lola, had expressed reservations about Toni. She'd wanted Abbie to wait a while before marrying him. But Abbie had become totally infatuated with the handsome Italian, who had gatecrashed one of her celebrity parties in Los Angeles. Eventually, wanting only for her daughter to be happy, Lola had given in. Abbie had also begged her father not to check out Toni's background, as he had wanted to, fearing retribution from Toni's Mafia connections. Now cracks were appearing in the fairy-tale relationship, and Abbie was left wondering whether Mommy might have been right after all.

Antonio poured himself a large bourbon, even though it was only mid-morning. Damn it! It was all going so well until they'd booked into this god-awful hotel. There was no way he was leaving without lawyers to protect his privacy — to fend off any awkward questions.

His phone rang. He looked at the screen. *No number.* Now what, for Christ's sake? He pressed the answer button. '*Pronto!*' he shouted, irritably. 'This is Count Antonio Di Vincenzo. What do you want?'

'Toni? Guess who this is.'

He recoiled at the woman's voice and tried hastily to end the call, but his hands were shaking. 'I don't know. Bugger off!'

'Yes, you do know — and don't cut me off or you'll be sorry.'

Antonio was thinking hard and fast. He couldn't have this conversation here — what if Abbie came back and overheard? This was meant to be the beginning of his affluent, idyllic new life, with everything he'd always wanted but couldn't afford. It seemed like all the fates had joined forces and were conspiring to ruin it.

'Wait a minute!' He slid open the blue-tinted panoramic window and went outside onto the balcony, breathing the salty air in shuddering, panicky gulps. He knew very well who was calling him — and why. He cursed the press and those bloody magazines, splashing his face all over the front covers for everyone to see. As for the Now to Zen, hadn't he told them he didn't want any publicity, when they booked in?

Reluctantly, he returned to his phone. 'How did you get this number, you interfering bitch? What do you want?'

'What do you think I want? And before you say anything, I know about Della.'

* * *

'Mother, I've just heard summat queer.' Fred Withenshaw had been taking a nap outside on their balcony.

Rita was dressing to go down to the Ritz Restaurant for lunch. 'You're always hearing something queer. It's that ancient hearing aid.'

'No, I don't mean queer noises, I mean a queer conversation. It came from the balcony upstairs.'

'Last time I looked, you were fast asleep. Like as not, you dreamed it.'

Fred shook his head. 'No, I definitely heard it.' He frowned. 'Who's in t'room above us?'

'It isn't a room,' said Rita. 'It's that posh honeymoon penthouse suite. That couple from California are in there — Antonio and Abbie something-or-other. He's the son of a count and she's heiress to a fortune.'

'Oh aye. The Italian fella that walks about wi' his nose in the air, like he's wearing a weskit made from the arse of his father's britches.'

'Dad, don't you dare say that in public! Whatever next!'

'Well, here's what was queer, Mother. It *were* his voice I heard, speaking on his phone. But then again, it weren't.'

'You're not making any sense, although that's nothing new. Either it was him or it wasn't.'

'It were his voice, all right, but the wrong lingo. He pretends to be Italian but he were talking cockney.'

'What, like on *EastEnders*?' Rita was interested now. 'I wonder why. What was he saying?'

'I didn't catch all of it, but what I did hear — when he got riled and started shouting — was that he wasn't going to give the lass on the other end any money. He threatened her with violence if she didn't leave him be.'

'How d'you know it were a lass on the other end?'

'Because he called her an "interfering bitch". You wouldn't call a lad that, would you?'

Rita nodded. 'I hope he isn't messing her about. His young wife, Abbie, I mean.'

'Why would he do that? Her dad's a multibillionaire. And they've only just got wed.'

'Yes, but you know what young men are like these days — can't keep it in their trousers. Your brother Raymond's eldest was having it off with the chief bridesmaid before the confetti had even settled.'

'I don't think you can compare Raymond's eldest to Italian nobility, Mother.'

'Is he, though? Italian, I mean. Or even a noble, come to that.' She wondered whether she should mention it to somebody. She didn't want to appear a busybody. On the other hand, the lass he'd married ought to know if there was something amiss. When they went down to the Ritz Restaurant for lunch, she found an opportunity to share her concerns.

* * *

Corrie had wanted to have lunch in the Grosvenor Room and Jack's vote had gone to the Cheerful Chophouse. They had compromised and were seated in the Ritz Restaurant.

'Cynthia and Carlene have gone home.' Corrie was perusing the menu, wondering whether to have the chilled pea velouté or a mango salad. 'Cyn says she's going to do a *Lysistrata* on George to punish him for not helping to get you out of DI Long's clutches. Carlene, ever the businesswoman, is anxious to take control of the Cuisine and Bistro again. Wasn't it good of them to come down? That's when you find out who your true friends are — when you're in trouble.'

'Right,' agreed Jack. 'To some people, a friend in need is a bloody liability. I thought I'd treat Bugsy to a few drinks in the bar later. He's going back to the station tomorrow. The MIT will be glad to see him.'

'I dare say Iris will be happy to have him home, too. I don't know what she'll make of his poor face, all cuts and bruises and two loose teeth. He winces every time he takes a deep breath, so his ribs must be damaged.'

'Battle scars,' declared Jack. 'A copper's badge of honour, in defence of law and order.'

'Those men are animals.' Corrie shook her head. 'What kind of human beings would do what they did to Eddie Clayton?'

'They forfeit the right to be treated as human beings when they join an OCG. Eddie double-crossed them, and he knew the risks if they caught up with him. He's committed similar atrocities on men, in his time.'

'Not just men,' said Corrie. 'The bastard murdered his wife.'

'Hmm,' said Jack.

* * *

As fate would have it, Rita and Corrie both needed to visit the ladies' at the same time. They were washing their hands in adjacent basins and commenting on the immaculate, fragrant loos, when Rita paused. 'Mrs Dawes, as you're a police officer's wife, could I ask your advice about something?'

'Yes, of course. Although I'm not sure I'm best qualified to offer anybody advice. I'm basically just a cook who occasionally meddles in police business and gets into scrapes, according to Jack.'

'It's about that young couple in t'honeymoon suite.'

'Toni and Abbie? Don't they make a lovely couple? So glamorous and perfectly matched,' enthused Corrie. 'They have such a wonderful life ahead of them.'

'I'm not so sure,' queried Rita. She explained that Fred had overheard Antonio on the phone to another woman. 'He were threatening the lass with violence if she didn't leave him alone.'

'I dare say a handsome, young, rich Italian noble is pursued by young women all the time, especially when his photograph is in all the society magazines and the media. I expect he was annoyed that the woman was bothering him on his honeymoon. I doubt if he really meant to harm her.'

'Yes, but why the cockney accent?'

Corrie raised her eyebrows. 'You didn't mention a cockney accent.'

'Didn't I? It was what surprised Fred. Why would an Italian count speak broad cockney on the phone, like an East Londoner?'

Why indeed? wondered Corrie. 'And Fred's sure it was Antonio Di Vincenzo?'

'Positive. I was just worried that he was cheating on his young wife, although I suppose it's none of my business — if he is.'

Corrie frowned. 'I'll mention it to Jack. There could be more to this than you and I realize.'

'Thank you, Mrs Dawes. I just needed to tell someone, to put my mind at rest.'

* * *

Back in the restaurant, Jack was ordering dessert. He fancied something decadent and chocolatey — the kind of thing he wasn't allowed at home. When Corrie reappeared after the extended toilet break, he hoped she didn't have an upset stomach. 'I've ordered you a fresh fruit salad, sweetheart. Is that OK?'

'Never mind that, now. Rita Withenshaw has just told me something curious.' She explained what Fred had overheard, including the cockney accent detail.

There was a long pause.

'Hmm,' said Jack.

'I wish you wouldn't do that,' complained Corrie. 'It's really annoying. I tell you something interesting and you just make that noise.'

'It's because I'm thinking.'

'Well, think out loud, please.'

'Not sure I can at the moment. I don't want to set a hare running, only to find out it's just a rabbit in disguise. I need to chew things over with Bugsy.'

'Now you're talking in riddles, which is even more annoying. And Bugsy's a bit deficient in the chewing department at present, so good luck with that.' She reached across the table and helped herself to a large spoonful of his chocolate fudge sundae.

CHAPTER TWENTY

While Toni was in this strange, angry mood, Abbie didn't fancy lunch in their suite. She couldn't understand why he was so bent out of shape. Everything had been cool when they first arrived at the spa. Then that woman had been murdered, the British cops were all over the place like hyped-up quarterbacks, and the vacation had bombed. OK, it was terrible that someone had been killed right there in the hotel, but what did it have to do with Toni that it should affect him that way? She didn't buy it. She decided to go for a walk on the shore to clear her head.

Ten minutes into her solitary stroll, she was overtaken by Louis running his lunchtime five miles. He jogged on the spot until she caught up. 'Hey there! I haven't seen you walking on the beach before.'

She gave him a tepid smile. 'That's because I haven't done it before.'

'Aren't you Abbie, the American lady from the honeymoon suite?'

She noticed that although he was still jogging on the spot, he wasn't at all breathless. This was one fit guy. 'Yep. But it doesn't feel much like a honeymoon right now.' She tried to focus on his face as he bobbed up and down. 'Could you quit jogging, please? It's making me dizzy.'

'Sorry.' He stopped and walked alongside her. 'I'm Louis, the spa fitness instructor and sports coach.'

'Yeah, I know. How ya doing, Louis?' She walked with her eyes downcast, looking at the sand.

He couldn't help noticing her perfect figure. Fitness was, after all, his profession. 'I can tell you work out, although I guess you haven't had much time for it, on honeymoon.' After he'd said the words, Louis immediately regretted it. Even to his careless ear, it sounded ill-mannered, but she didn't seem offended.

'Back home in LA, I work out every day. I have my own fully equipped gym.'

'Wow!' Louis was impressed.

'I'm very lucky. I have great parents.'

He hesitated. 'If you don't mind me saying, you don't seem very happy for someone who's very lucky, has great parents and is on their honeymoon. Is there something I can do?'

'No thanks, Louis. You're one of the good guys, for sure, but this is something I have to fix myself.'

'OK, but if I can help, just say the word.' He carried on with his run and left her to her thoughts but made a mental note to keep an eye on Count Antonio Di Vincenzo, just in case.

* * *

That evening, Jack went next door to the Stone's Throw for a drink with Bugsy. The relaxed ambience of its cocktail lounge seemed more conducive to normal conversation than the somewhat constrained atmosphere of the Now to Zen. And he wanted to avoid the possibility of being overheard. By the time he arrived, Bugsy had already got the drinks in, and some munchies, of the kind his loose teeth could manage. He was sitting in a comfortable chair to ease his bruised ribs.

'How are you, Bugsy? The face is looking better.'

'I sent the team a pic, just to show I'd been suffering for the cause and not just fannying about on a freebie holiday.'

He grinned. 'Young Aled reckoned the smack in the mouth was an improvement, cheeky sod.' He took a long swig of his beer and winced as it swilled around his cut lips. 'Where's Mrs Dawes tonight?'

'She's booked an evening session in the steam room, followed by a massage, so I shan't be missed. She wants to lose some weight.'

'Why? A skinny chef isn't much of a recommendation.'

'I agree, but you know Corrie, once she's made up her mind about something — which is one of the things I wanted to run past you.'

'Fire away, guv.'

'Have you given any more thought to the murder of Della Clayton?'

Bugsy put down his glass. 'I'm guessing you don't think Eddie Clayton killed her.'

Trust good old Bugsy to hit the nail squarely on the head, thought Jack. 'No. In fact, I'm pretty sure he didn't. Trouble is, if he didn't do it, who did? And why?'

'We know that Clayton, aka Sir Marcus Wellbeloved, had agreed to meet Della in the twilight whirlpool room that night. He was carrying the gun that he'd used to shoot a copper. I'm assuming he went there intending to kill her.'

Jack nodded. 'OK, so why didn't he shoot her?'

'Exactly what I was wondering,' confirmed Bugsy. 'Why risk a dodgy electrocution that could easily have gone wrong? Clive searched on the PNC and asked the NCA for everything that we had on Clayton. Pretty handy with torture weapons of all kinds but nothing about electrical skills.'

Jack leaned forward in his chair. 'Tell you what I reckon — Clayton was on the run with the money that he'd swiped from the gang. Probably planning to leg it abroad once the fuss had died down and the all-ports warning was lifted. Meanwhile, Della had fallen on hard times and somehow tracked him down. She demanded her share, or she'd tell the gang where he was.'

'And we know that by that time, she'd already shopped him. Probably forced to. Remember, the ends of her little fingers were missing,' added Bugsy. 'That's why they were waiting for him outside the hotel. They'd have been more careful this time, having already snatched Tim Bennett by mistake.'

'Right. Anyway, she arranged to meet him late at night, in the whirlpool room. Corrie reckons she slipped in, unnoticed, in a bogus staff uniform. He booked in beforehand as Sir Marcus, so as not to arouse suspicion, but when he got to the pool pod, she was lying there, already dead. He chucked in the gun because he didn't want to be found with it, in the event of a search, and hurried back to his room. His plan was to pack up and leave straight away. But before he could, Corrie and I found the body and all hell broke loose.'

'With you so far, guv, but why a posh hotel and spa? It isn't the sort of place that either of them would normally choose. Why not a seedy café or pub in London — their usual haunts? No need for the cloak-and-dagger stuff, then. He could have just taken her down a dark alley and put a bullet in her head. Happens a lot with organized crime.'

Jack sipped his whisky. 'Good point. If it was Della who chose the location, and I believe it was, she must have had another reason for wanting to be there.'

'That's what Mrs Dawes and I thought. And the "other reason" was probably the person who killed her. It's a bugger. Now they're both dead and we don't have a lead of any kind.' He thought for a bit. 'Clive pulled in a copy of Della's post-mortem, in case there was something DI Long had missed. It recorded that she'd had a baby when she was very young. That would make the child in its twenties, now. It's a bit of a leap but what if, somehow, she'd traced the kid to the spa, and she'd come to find him or her? It'd have to be a member of staff. Guests come and go.'

'So do the staff,' said Jack. 'I believe these places have quite a high turnover.'

'Who's been there a reasonable length of time, in that age group?'

Jack thought. 'Rainbow, Kelly-Anne, Louis, lots of the practitioners. It wouldn't be David, the Jefferson software engineer — apparently his mother rings him regularly. I don't know about Meredith. I suppose we could check, now she's in custody. It's a hell of a long shot, Bugsy.'

'Yeah, I know. I'm clutching at straws, Jack. It worries me that they've just accepted that Eddie killed Della, then closed the case without further investigation. It's just too fast and convenient and the evidence doesn't stack up.'

'You're telling me!' exclaimed Jack. 'It wasn't that long ago that they had me in the frame.'

'So what next? Do we just give up?'

'Not yet,' said Jack. 'At lunchtime, Corrie had a gossip in the loo, like women do, with a lady called Rita Withenshaw. She and her husband, Fred, have the room below the honeymoon suite.'

'That'll be the Jefferson heiress and the Italian count.'

'Right. Well, Fred was out on his balcony and he thought he heard the count talking with a cockney accent, threatening a woman on the phone. Telling her to leave him alone or she'd regret it.'

'That's weird,' said Bugsy. 'My Iris has been following their society wedding and honeymoon plans in her celebrity magazines. Big pictures all over the covers. He's supposed to come from a long line of Sicilian nobles. So where did the cockney come from? Fred was sure about it, I suppose?'

'Positive. Rita was worried for Abbie — she thought Antonio may have been cheating on her. How about you stay down here another day and we check it out? It's probably nothing at all to do with the Clayton murder, but my copper's nose is twitching.'

'Yeah. Della's last known address was a flat in Braxton Tower in the East End of London. Worth a bit of a nudge, guv.' Bugsy swigged the last dregs of his beer. 'I believe it's your round, and I reckon I could manage a pork pie, if I cut it up small.'

* * *

Corrie had been in the steam room for some time. She looked down at her thighs — white, moist and translucent. She grinned to herself. *A wedge of lemon and some parsley sauce and they'd pass for a couple of giant cod fillets.* While she'd been steaming, she'd had time to think about what Rita had told her at lunchtime. It was certainly curious. She doubted that Jack would consider it important enough to check out, and besides, she'd told him he mustn't do any more detecting. There was nothing to stop *her*, though. She didn't like to think of a young lady so in love and so recently married being cheated on by her husband. Jack would say she shouldn't interfere but the only thing necessary for evil to triumph — she half-recalled the quote — is for good men to do nothing, or something like that.

On her way back to her room, she saw her chance. A white-gloved waiter was wheeling a trolley of dirty crockery towards the kitchens. It was obviously from the honeymoon suite as it had an empty bottle of their special champagne and the wreckage of a couple of lobsters. It also had a crystal bourbon glass. Corrie was pretty sure that would have been Antonio's. As the waiter passed her, she squealed, 'Oh my god! There's a rat!'

The waiter jumped. 'Where, madam?'

'Over there, behind that plant pot.' Corrie pointed.

He left the trolley and rushed to look. Swiftly, Corrie picked up the bourbon glass between fingertip and thumb and stuffed it into the pocket of her bathrobe.

The young waiter returned. 'I couldn't see anything, madam. Was it a big rat?'

'Er . . . no, not really. Not much bigger than a mouse, in fact. Hardly a rat at all.'

The waiter looked sceptical. 'I'll get maintenance to do a pest-control sweep of this floor.'

'Right . . . thank you.' She hurried off. Tomorrow, she'd get her friend Noz to test the glass for prints and run them through the police database, just to be on the safe side. Jack didn't need to know anything about it.

CHAPTER TWENTY-ONE

Once the police embargo had been lifted, guests had checked out of the Now to Zen in droves, until it was virtually empty. Despite waiving the fees in an attempt to compensate for the disruption, people were ill at ease. They'd signed up for an oasis of calm, and instead, they had found themselves in a quagmire of crime.

'You'd think they'd be glad of some free extra days in a luxurious spa like this,' complained Dick.

'Be realistic,' urged Penny. 'Who'd want to spend a relaxing holiday in a place where people are being murdered?'

'We still have our Now to Zen poster couple in the honeymoon suite. That should count for something.'

'Not for much longer,' said Penny. 'I've been informed that Jefferson's private plane from LA has landed at Gatwick. The lawyers will be here very soon.'

Dick was puzzled. 'I don't understand why Count Di Vincenzo insisted on waiting for them before he would check out. His wife was keen to move on to Monaco as soon as possible.'

'Who knows?' pondered Penny. 'I expect he has his reasons.'

* * *

Jack was in the Stone's Throw, discussing the possible causes of his 'twitching nose' with Bugsy. Back at Kings Richington station, Gemma had explained to the chief super why Acting Detective Inspector Malone continued to be absent. Her gruesome description of Bugsy's imminent dental implant, drilled into his jawbone, to replace the root of his painful tooth had been graphic enough to prevent Garwood from asking any further questions. Clive had been sleuthing online, but so far had failed to find anything relating to the long line of Di Vincenzo Sicilian nobles to which Antonio claimed to belong. More significantly, he could find no personal history or back story of any kind prior to the much-publicized engagement to Abbie Jefferson. He related this anomaly to Bugsy, who discussed it with Jack.

'He can't have come down with yesterday's rain, guv,' reasoned Bugsy. 'D'you reckon he's changed his identity to escape from the Mafia? A kind of Italian version of witness protection?'

Jack shook his head. 'If that were the case, why would he persist with the Italian angle? He'd be safer pretending to be a cockney, now we know he can carry off the accent. My nose tells me this bloke has form, if not in the US, then in the UK. If only we could get hold of his prints, I'm sure they'd give us some answers.'

* * *

When Corrie gave Noz the bourbon glass to check for prints, she hadn't anticipated such startling results. When he came to report what he'd found, she took him into the Caribbean Lounge, little realizing that in the hotel next door, Jack and Bugsy were working along much the same lines of inquiry, but with a far less dramatic outcome.

'There was only one set of prints on the glass, Mrs Dawes.'

'Please, you must call me Corrie, if I can call you Noz. That would be because the clean glass would have gone through the hotel's powerful dishwasher before Antonio handled it. The waiter was wearing white gloves to take it away, so we can be pretty sure the prints are Count Antonio's.'

'Oh, I think we can be certain of that,' declared Noz. 'Except his name isn't Count Antonio Di Vincenzo — it's plain old Tony Vincent.'

'I knew it!' spluttered Corrie. 'He's dodgy, isn't he?'

'Not half. He was born in Hackney, not Sicily. He owes his Mediterranean good looks and convincing accent to an Italian grandfather who ran an ice cream shop in the East End. Tony's got a charge sheet as long as your arm. Nothing major — mostly petty theft, dealing drugs and assault. Few stretches inside. Bit of a temper on him, apparently. Plenty of accounts of domestic assault. Which brings me to the really interesting part. Last time we lifted him, he was living in a flat in Braxton Tower, a high-rise, East London tower block with a wife called Sharon and two small children. I checked that the marriage is genuine but there's no record of any divorce.'

'The swine!' exclaimed Corrie. 'He isn't really married to Abbie Jefferson at all, is he?'

'Doesn't look like it. There are also child maintenance arrears in respect of another woman and considerable gambling debts.'

Corrie never ceased to be amazed that men got away with this kind of behaviour. If he'd been her husband, she'd have served up his gonads as croquettes on toast before throwing him out. 'Did he work at all?'

'The only job on record was as a "roadie" with the Hackney Heroes — a local rock band.'

Corrie raised an eyebrow. 'No doubt because it got him away from the wife and kids, for long periods.'

'I did some digging to see what I could find out about the band. There were five of them in the line-up and they did quite well, initially. They performed at several gigs around the UK and abroad, including a couple of music festivals. Tony was the sound engineer, in charge of the electronics. He travelled with them to the US to manage the audio and lighting equipment for their concerts. When the band finally broke up and returned to the UK, he stayed on in the States.'

'I'm not surprised,' said Corrie, 'with all those women at home, chasing him for money. Never mind the heavy brigade after him for his gambling debts.'

'He disappeared off the UK radar after that. I'm guessing that's when he reinvented himself as Count Antonio Di Vincenzo.'

Corrie frowned. 'According to the gossip magazines, and I quote from memory, *Antonio met Abbie after gate-crashing one of her celebrity parties in LA. She fell for "the handsome Sicilian" immediately and they became inseparable*. What a rat!'

'The part that concerns me,' continued Noz, 'is that he must have pretty good electrical skills.'

Corrie could see where this was leading. 'Enough to electrify a whirlpool?'

'That's what I was thinking.'

'But what motive would he have had for wanting Della Clayton dead? Corrie wondered. 'How would he have met her? Was she even the intended target?'

'I don't know the answer to any of those questions. And soon, we won't be able to find out, because the Jefferson lawyers are coming to get him out. He'll have an impenetrable ring of legal protection around him.'

'We can't let that happen, Noz. I doubt if your DI Long will be interested in doing anything.'

'She isn't my DI any longer. She's been suspended while the IOPC investigate the mishandling of the Clayton case. They haven't found a replacement, yet.'

'In that case, I think we should tell Jack what you've found. He'll know what action to take.'

* * *

Corrie and Noz arrived in the lounge of the Stone's Throw at the point where Jack and Bugsy were wishing they had Antonio's fingerprints.

Corrie did away with time-wasting preamble. 'Jack, you need to listen to this. Noz has some vital information.'

Jack and Bugsy listened to the Tony Vincent saga in silence.

'Blimey!' exclaimed Bugsy, when Noz had finished. 'I didn't see that coming, did you, guv?'

'Not entirely.' Jack was thoughtful. 'How did you manage to get Vincent's prints?'

'Er . . .' Noz looked at Corrie.

'I pinched a glass,' she confessed, 'and I asked Noz to check it out. Now, don't come over all "pursed lips", Jack. Somebody had to do something before it was too late.'

'I agree. I just wish it wasn't always you breaking the law. You really should leave it to the criminals. They're so much better at it — they don't get caught as often as you.'

'What do we do now, sir?' asked Noz.

Jack thought about it. 'At the very least, bigamy is still a crime, punishable by up to seven years in the nick. We can hold him for that, while we investigate his possible involvement in the murder of Della Clayton.'

'What about the team of American lawyers? Won't they try to hustle him out of the country?' Corrie worried.

'They can try, but when they discover Vincent's real identity and his list of criminal activities, I think it will put them on the back foot — at least long enough for us to question him about the murder.'

'Do you fancy him for it, guv?' asked Bugsy.

'Definitely. Now we know that both Della and Tony Vincent had lived, at some time, in the Braxton Tower flats in Hackney, there's a slim chance we have a motive.'

Bugsy nodded. 'His face was all over my Iris's women's magazines, as well as details about starting their honeymoon in Brightsea. What if Della recognized him and put the screws on? We know she was down on her luck. She thought she'd touch him for few quid. Pay up or she tells his new wife that he hasn't got rid of his old one — never mind the kids.'

Corrie wasn't sure. 'I thought she'd gone to the Now to Zen to meet Eddie Clayton and demand money from him?'

'She could have arranged both meetings,' suggested Noz. 'A woman in her position can never have too much cash.'

'Pity she never got to spend any of it,' said Bugsy.

'Maybe it wasn't money she wanted from Vincent,' mused Corrie. 'Perhaps it was something else. I can't imagine what, though.'

Jack summed up. 'Tony Vincent had motive — to stop Della from ruining his new life of luxury. He had means — the skills to engineer the electrocution. And he had opportunity — free access to the twilight whirlpools.'

'I think you should nick him and squeeze him, till the pips squeak,' urged Corrie.

'That's a little lurid, darling, but I agree he has some serious questions to answer. What I'm not sure about is whose job it is to ask them.'

'It definitely won't be DI Long, sir,' emphasized Noz. 'She's on indefinite gardening leave.'

Every police-infused fibre in Jack's body wanted to take over this case. Even Corrie had changed her mind about not letting him work on holiday, now that she felt outraged at the way both Abbie and Della had been treated. Tony Vincent couldn't be allowed to escape abroad without investigation. But two factors mitigated it — police protocol and Chief Superintendent Garwood.

* * *

As it turned out, the situation was rapidly resolved. Jack's phone rang.

'Inspector Dawes?' Jack recognized the voice of Nancy, Garwood's newly acquired personal assistant. 'I have Chief Superintendent Garwood for you.' There was a click, then Garwood came on the line.

'Dawes? I won't ask if you're enjoying your holiday, I understand it's been a little . . . fraught.'

You can say that again, thought Jack. *I was arrested and you didn't support me. Even worse, you actually believed I might be corrupt.* 'We've had a few ups and downs, sir.'

'Yes, well . . .' He coughed, embarrassed. 'I've had a call from the chief superintendent of Brightsea CID. It seems he has received new information regarding the Della Clayton murder, which casts doubt on the guilt of Eddie Clayton. This means the killer could still be at large. He has shared this information with the IPOC and they want the case reopened.'

'Very sensible, sir.' Jack knew what was coming but he wasn't going to make it easy for him.

Garwood began to bluster as he always did when he felt he was on uncertain ground. His attitude to policing was that you never openly or directly admit that you've done something wrong while you're in a leadership position, or you just open yourself to criticism from all sides. 'I have agreed that since you are on the spot, so to speak, and have had close involvement in the case, you are best placed to take charge as the senior investigating officer. I don't see any conflict of interest arising.'

Close involvement? argued Jack, silently. *I nearly got sent down for it! Involvement doesn't get much closer than that.*

'Take as long as you need, Dawes. Under the circumstances, I have obtained financial clearance for you to stay in the hotel, with your wife, while the investigation is ongoing. You have authority to take over from tomorrow. Is all that clear?'

'Yes, sir. Perfectly clear, sir.'

'I believe a DS Larry Bristow will be coming to assist you.'

'Ah.' Jack was doubtful. 'I'm not sure that's such a good idea, sir. DS Bristow was on the original investigation with DI Long. I feel it needs a fresh pair of eyes — a completely new approach without any preconceived bias. Would it be possible for me to have DS Malone for a few days?'

'That could be problematic. Malone is on sick leave with severe dental complications involving—' he swallowed hard — 'metal screws in his jaw.'

'I'm sure if you asked him, sir, he'd manage to struggle down here, to assist me.'

'All right. I'll get Nancy to give him a ring. But it will be his decision, and I can't be responsible if his health suffers as a result.'

'No, of course not, sir. Thank you, sir.'

Jack switched off his phone and punched the air. *Good man, Noz!* He would have been the source of the new information finding its way to the Brightsea chief super.

Now we can sort this case, Jack thought, *before anyone else gets hurt.*

CHAPTER TWENTY-TWO

It was early morning. Corrie had got up to pop to the loo and glanced out of the window. 'Jack, they're here.'

A cavalcade of black limousines with tinted windows was drawing up outside the Now to Zen.

'It's the team of Jefferson lawyers.'

'Blimey, that was quick.' Jack was pulling on his trousers. 'They weren't scheduled to arrive until this afternoon. They're obviously intending to sneak the couple out, without attracting the attention of the paparazzi or the cops.'

'I still think you should have pounced on Vincent last night. You could at least have tackled him about the bigamy — the two-timing, avaricious, murdering swine!'

'No, I couldn't, my little avenging angel.' He kissed the top of her head. 'I didn't have authority on this patch until today. But I'm going down to do it now. Proving he's a killer will hopefully come later.' He handed Corrie his phone. 'Give Bugsy a ring. Tell him to call for uniformed backup and DC Nosworthy, then meet me downstairs in the foyer.'

Bugsy went from snoring to fully dressed in a matter of minutes. It was a skill he had acquired over the years. He joined Jack in the Now to Zen lobby just as the couple was leaving. They were shielded by several dark-suited lawyers, all talking on their phones, while uniformed porters loaded their luggage onto revolving baggage carts.

You have to hand it to the Jefferson outfit, thought Jack. *They don't do things by halves.*

He pushed his way through them until he was facing Vincent, then he put a restraining hand on his shoulder. With long-practised ease, Bugsy slid in behind the suspect, to cover any attempt at escape.

'Tony Vincent,' intoned Jack, 'I am arresting you on suspicion of bigamy, in direct contravention of Section 57 of the Offences against the Person Act, 1861. Sergeant Malone, read him his rights.'

At first, there was a moment of eerie silence, while this information was processed. Then pandemonium broke out with everybody shouting at once. Bugsy's voice could be heard, booming out the caution. The lawyers were clearly in total disarray. They had been hired to get Count Antonio Di Vincenzo and his wife out of the UK and onto Jefferson's private plane to Monaco. The fact that Carter Jefferson's daughter might not be the guy's legal wife was a complication they hadn't foreseen.

Abbie was horrified. She threw her arms around her beloved and clung to him. 'Tonino, my darling, why is he calling you Tony Vincent? This is a mistake, isn't it? Tell him!'

He shoved her away, roughly. 'Of course it's a mistake,' Vincent bluffed, still in an Italian accent. 'I don't know what you're talking about.' He attempted to push past Jack. '*Andare via!* Get out of my way, we have a plane waiting.'

Bugsy blocked him with his not inconsiderable bulk — a manoeuvre that had proved effective on many similar occasions. 'Come quietly, sir. I don't want to handcuff you in front of the lady.'

Vincent was belligerent, but at the same time, clearly terrified. His worst fears were coming true. 'You have no proof. This is an outrage.' He appealed to the lawyers. 'Get me out of here!'

'The entry held by the General Register Office confirms your marriage to Sharon Vincent, née Jones, in the London borough of Hackney, ten years ago,' Jack replied. 'It is sufficient legal proof, sir.'

'But even if that's true, it doesn't count, does it?' Abbie was sobbing and desperate. 'Toni married me in California.'

Jack felt sorry for her, as did Corrie, who had been observing from a distance. 'I'm afraid your lawyers will confirm, Miss Jefferson, that a person cannot get married in the United States if he is already married, no matter where the first marriage took place.' There was no way Jack could soften the blow, but now was not the time to tell her about the children, legitimate and otherwise. No doubt she would find out eventually.

By now, uniformed backup and DC Nosworthy had arrived. Jack motioned to them to take Vincent to Brightsea station for questioning. Anxious to protect their jobs, the Jefferson lawyers stepped back, realizing they had no authority to prevent the arrest. Their next step would be to contact Carter Jefferson to find out if he wished them to defend Vincent against the charge of bigamy. God knew how. Unless they could cook up some kind of prenup Mickey Mouse divorce, they were onto a loser.

* * *

Tony Vincent's brain was buzzing like a beehive with fears of what else the police would charge him with once he was in custody. This man Dawes was smart. It wouldn't take him long to question Sharon, and now that she couldn't screw money out of him, the stupid cow would tell the coppers everything, hoping for some kind of compo. If he didn't get out of here *now*, he'd be facing a lot longer inside than a few years for bigamy. There was only one solution.

As Bugsy would admit later, it had been a mistake not to handcuff Vincent. When they got him outside to the police van, he asked if he might kiss his sobbing 'wife' goodbye. Jack nodded to DC Nosworthy and the constables stood back to allow Abbie to get close to him.

Vincent saw his chance to escape. When Abbie tried to hold on to him, he hit her — a vicious blow that knocked her down and drew blood. Then, before the officers could grab him, he ran out of the hotel forecourt and down towards the beach.

He had no idea where he was heading but he'd think of something, once he'd shaken off the filth. He dodged and jinked, but they were fitter than he expected. They were closing in on either side of him, until there was only one avenue of escape left. He ran into the sea.

The tide was in and he was a poor swimmer. He crashed through the waves, feeling the strong undercurrent pulling at his legs. Soon he was out of his depth and gasping for breath.

Luckily, Louis was out for his morning run along the shore. It took just a split second for him to sum up the situation. Count Antonio What's-his-name was running from the police. He wasn't surprised — he'd always known the bloke was shifty. It was Louis's duty to carry out a citizen's arrest, wasn't it? He swam out, with effortlessly powerful strokes, easily overtaking the struggling constables, who were in pursuit wearing full uniform. He reached Vincent, thrashing about and half-drowned, and hauled him, dripping and spluttering, from the water.

'Come on, you miserable little runt. The cops want a word with you.' He dragged him back up the beach by the scruff of his neck to where Jack, Bugsy and several sodden constables were waiting. Choking from Louis's vice-like grip on his collar, like an animal snared in a noose, Vincent tried to swing a punch at him, but Bugsy pulled his arms behind his back and slapped on the cuffs.

'Don't be daft, son. You don't want to get into a fight with him — he'll slaughter you.' He handed Vincent over to the uniformed constables. 'Put the Count of Monte Cristo in the van, please.'

* * *

Soaked through from his impromptu swim, Louis squelched his way back to the hotel and his room to shower and change. The lobby was busy with the lawyers on their phones, reporting what had taken place and requesting urgent instructions. In one corner, Abbie was sitting on a couch with Corrie, who was attempting to staunch the blood pouring from her nose and mouth and rapidly soaking into her top.

Louis stopped beside them, creating a growing puddle of water on the carpet. He crouched down to look more closely at her injured face. 'Did he do that?'

Unable to speak, Abbie nodded, sadly. Her brave new world had fallen apart in a matter of minutes.

'She won't let me call an ambulance,' said Corrie. 'He hit her so hard, Louis. I'm sure she needs someone to look at her injuries. Her jaw could be fractured and I think her nose is broken.'

'I've got qualifications in sports injuries and I'm a trained first response volunteer.' Louis took Abbie's hand. 'Will you let me see if I can help? Just until your parents can arrange for private medics to come and pick you up.'

She nodded. Louis led her gently away to his treatment room next to the gym. If nothing else, he could make her more comfortable and prevent any infection. Inside, he was fuming. What sort of bloke hits a woman? He wished, now, that he'd given the cowardly git a good hiding before handing him over.

* * *

'Ee, I'll go to t'foot of our stairs!' exclaimed Fred. He'd been watching the action from their window. 'What do you make of that, Mother? The police have arrested that arty-farty Italian fella.'

Rita crossed her arms. Her mouth was turned down at the corners, indicating her disapproval. 'I never warmed to him. Like as not, he's been messing that lass around right from the cake-cutting. Didn't I tell you, Dad? He's just like your brother Raymond's eldest.'

'I don't think the police can arrest you for a bit o' han-ky-panky on t'side, Mother. Otherwise, most of the lads down t'Ferret and Trouserleg would be in a cell. He must have done summat worse than that.'

'Well, that nice Inspector Dawes is in charge now. He'll get the truth out of him. That last woman didn't have a clue.'

'You mean her with a face like a penguin with piles? Reckon you're right there, Mother. Pity we're going home at t'weekend. It's been reet lively. Can we have breakfast now? I could eat a horse between two bread vans.'

* * *

Dorothy Buncombe had been similarly fascinated by the activity, especially Louis's part in it. The sisters were also returning home at the weekend and Dorothy was disappointed that she hadn't been able to engage in any activities with Louis — or any other man, for that matter. Sir Marcus Wellbeloved had turned out to be a fake. Not only that but a criminal, too. Maybe even a murderer. She sighed.

'What's up with you?' asked Peggy.

'It's been a waste of time and money, this holiday.'

'No, it hasn't,' contradicted Peggy. 'I've had some wonderful workouts on the Downs and my back is much better.'

'I came here hoping I could have some wonderful workouts too, but it's been a dead loss. Even Louis's 'Stay Young and Beautiful' classes were a disappointment.'

Peggy patted her shoulder. 'Never mind, Dotty. I expect he felt threatened by your raw physicality. Speaking of which, don't forget we're hiring a new groom when we get back to the stables. It'll need someone with muscles to handle Saracen.'

'Yes, it will, won't it?' Dorothy smiled. 'And I noticed that one of the applicants is called Bond — Jimmy Bond.'

* * *

Jack rubbed his hands together. 'OK, gentlemen, let's have some breakfast, then we'll question Vincent down at Brightsea station, after he's been processed. This time, I believe we'll get the definitive answer to the murder mystery of Della Clayton, our "lady in black".'

'I'll set up an incident room, sir,' offered DC Nosworthy.

'After that, Noz, I'd like you to get yourself to Braxton Tower and take a statement from Sharon Vincent. I could get the local lads to do it, but I think it will be more effective coming from you, since you're familiar with the case and on the ball. We need to find out if there was any connection between Tony Vincent and Della Clayton.'

'Yes, sir.' Noz was pleased and keen to get started. Now the investigation would be carried out properly and he would be part of it.

* * *

Jack and Corrie were on their way to the Cheerful Chophouse for a swift egg on toast. There was work to be done.

Kelly-Anne fell into step beside Jack. 'Hello, Jack. I'm Kelly-Anne, your—'

'Spa buddy. Yes, I know. What can I do for you, Kelly-Anne? Only, we're a bit pushed for time.'

'I wondered if you could tell me when Count Di Vincenzo will be back.'

Jack was blunt. 'Not for a very long time, if I have anything to do with it.'

'Oh dear!' She chewed her lip. 'I'm not sure what to do now.'

'Why do you want to know?' asked Corrie.

'Because he promised me a part in his next film if I helped him. He didn't want anyone to know who he was, because the *paparapizza* follow him around and young women keep throwing themselves at him. He's a very famous Italian film director.'

163

'What did he want from you in return?' Corrie hardly dared to ask. This poor girl wasn't safe out on her own.

'Oh, not what you're thinking. Nothing like that. Although he wouldn't have been the first man to offer me an acting job in return for . . . you know . . . favours. You can't trust them, can you? Men, I mean. Not you, Jack. I trust you *explicitly*. It's just that Mrs Hawkins said she saw him being bundled into a police van. I suppose that was for his own protection from the press, was it?'

'Something like that,' said Jack, who was now taking an interest. 'What was it he wanted you to do, Kelly-Anne?'

'It was more what he didn't want me to do, really. Do you remember the other night, when you, me and Mrs Dawes found that dead woman?'

'Yes, we remember it very well.' Corrie wondered if she'd ever forget that twisted face and those sightless eyes.

'Well, I was on my way to the Dorchester Room, to take you to the twilight whirlpool after your dinner, when I bumped into him on the stairs. He was hurrying back to the honeymoon spa suite, which wasn't *auspicious* in itself. It was what he had in his hand that was odd. When he saw me staring at it, he put it back in his trousers.'

'What did he have in his hand, Kelly-Anne?' Once again, Corrie could hardly bring herself to ask.

'It looked like one of those things you use to drive screws in.'

'A screwdriver?' suggested Corrie.

'Yes, that's it. I expect he wanted to adjust something in his room, although we have maintenance people for that. And he was carrying a really cheap, scuzzy-looking mobile phone. He *congealed* it in his pocket with the screwdriver, as soon as I saw it. I wondered what a famous film director would be doing with that, when he could afford any smart-phone he liked. He asked me not to mention seeing him, as his wife would be cross. She didn't like him leaving her alone at night. Then he said I was a very pretty girl and he had a part for me in his next film.' She paused, recollecting.

'It was a lively old night — apart from the dead woman, of course. She wasn't at all lively. But half an hour later, I saw Sir Marcus. He was dashing back to his room, as well.'

Jack was trying not to explode with frustration. Corrie could hear him taking deep breaths. Making an effort to speak calmly and kindly, he asked, 'Why didn't you say something about this before, Kelly-Anne?'

'Because I promised not to.' Her surprised expression implied that it went without saying, didn't it? A promise was a promise. 'And besides, we're supposed to be discreet. Lots of married gentlemen visit the massage practitioners' rooms in the middle of the night. Mrs Hawkins says it's part of their treatment programme.'

Oh crikey! thought Corrie. *Not only have I brought Jack to a place where people are murdered but it's a high-class knocking shop on the side. Wait till Cynthia and Carlene find out. I'll never live it down.*

Jack explained gently, 'Kelly-Anne, promises don't count during a police inquiry.'

'Don't they?'

'No. And I'm sorry, but this man isn't a film director or a count or Italian. He's a liar and a cheat.'

'Oh.' She looked crestfallen. 'I thought it was too good to be true.'

Jack put his arm around her, vowing to make life as unpleasant as the law would allow for Tony Vincent. The man's *raison d'être* was to cause disappointment and devastation to any young woman unfortunate enough to cross his path. He would also get the SOCOs to do a sweep of the honeymoon suite, now that Abbie had been moved to another apartment. With any luck, they might locate the items Kelly-Anne mentioned. 'I'll need you to come to Brightsea Police Station and make a statement about what you've just told me. Is that all right?'

'Yes, of course, Jack, if that's what you want.' She turned to Corrie. 'I've never been to a police station. What do you think I should wear?'

CHAPTER TWENTY-THREE

When he was told of the alarming chain of events — and in particular Tony Vincent's bigamy charge — Carter Jefferson instructed his team of lawyers to return to California. On no account were they to provide any kind of legal representation to the man who had cruelly duped their daughter. He and Lola were flying over in person to fetch Abbie home after her ordeal. She was understandably devastated to discover that the man she had adored, the man she had married in a lavish celebration with every extravagance that money could buy, was a charlatan and a fake. As far as Carter was concerned, his 'son-in-law' was on his own. He trusted that the British courts would throw the book at him. If not, he would have him extradited and tried in a US court. At that stage, Jefferson was unaware of the much more serious crime of which Vincent was suspected.

* * *

The Brightsea Police Station interview room smelled of stale sweat, disinfectant and the sausage rolls that Bugsy had brought in a burger box for later. He'd reckoned this interview would take some time and his borderline pastry addiction might kick in at any moment.

DC Nosworthy was on his way to London to interview Vincent's wife, so a uniformed constable stood on guard by the door. He'd been told that the suspect was a potential bolter and to be on the alert. Another constable was stationed outside, chosen for his impressive proportions and his fierce, 'he won't get past me, guv' demeanour.

Instead of his team of shit-hot American lawyers, Vincent found himself represented by the station's duty solicitor, a wizened little man who was looking forward to retirement in six months' time. He'd already decided, having read the bigamy charges presented by the police, that this particular client was on a hiding to nothing, even without Sharon Vincent's statement, which would no doubt put the lid on it. No point in knocking himself out on a no-hoper. Now that Carter Jefferson had withdrawn his support, there wouldn't be any money in it. From what he could elicit, his client had no significant funds of his own, relying solely on those of his 'wife', to which she had now blocked his access. Who could blame her? The solicitor joined the ranks of the 'don't look up, just keep scribbling' school of legal representation. With any luck, he'd be home by teatime.

'Well, this is a hell of a fall from grace, isn't it, Tony?' Bugsy smiled, genially. 'Son of an Italian nobleman, Count Antonio Di Vincenzo reduced to petty crook and bigamist, Tony Vincent. After crashing down from that height, I'm surprised you haven't got a nosebleed.'

'No comment.' His tone was sulky and defiant. He chewed gum with his mouth open, his jaws chomping mindlessly.

'Are you denying the charge of bigamy, Mr Vincent?' asked Jack politely.

'No point, is there?' He had slipped back into his native cockney in barely a heartbeat.

'Why did you marry Abbie Jefferson when you were already married to Sharon Jones?'

He shrugged. 'Forgot, didn't I?'

'How could you forget you were married? You had two children with her.' Bugsy couldn't believe this bloke was expecting to be taken seriously.

'Yeah, well, I was in the States, wasn't I? Didn't think it mattered there.'

Bugsy sneered. 'You're not that stupid, Mr Vincent. You knew very well you weren't free to marry but you couldn't pass up a chance to get on the Jefferson gravy train, could you? But you needed a dashing new identity to do it. Abbie Jefferson would never have fallen for a wide boy from Hackney with a wife and two kids.'

'It's not illegal to call yourself by a different name.' Vincent looked for confirmation from his solicitor, who ignored him and carried on scribbling.

'The law allows you to assume any name provided its use is not calculated to deceive or to inflict pecuniary loss,' said Bugsy. 'That's exactly what you intended to do, so I think we can rule out that argument, don't you?'

'Why did you run?' asked Jack. 'It was a risky strategy, running into the sea, when you knew you were a poor swimmer.'

'Didn't want to do time, did I?'

'Surely a few years for bigamy is a better option than drowning?' suggested Jack. 'You see, I think you ran because you guessed we had discovered a much worse crime — a crime that could earn you a life sentence.'

'I don't know what you mean.' Vincent's face drained of colour.

Bugsy stood up, hands in his pockets, and sauntered nonchalantly around to Vincent's side of the table. He stood behind him. 'Tell us about Della Clayton, Tony.'

Vincent glanced nervously over his shoulder. 'Wasn't she the old tart who drowned herself in one of the whirlpools?' The masticating jaws worked even faster.

Bugsy put his hands on the back of Vincent's chair. 'Did you do it, Tony? Did you short-circuit the wires to the underwater lights? Did you push Della in the pool and electrocute her, to shut her up? We have a witness who says she saw you coming from the twilight whirlpool room, carrying a screwdriver and a cheap phone, probably Della's, on the night of her murder. We've got a team of forensics officers turning over your spa suite as we speak, and they're going to find where you've hidden them. How will you explain that?'

The duty solicitor's prostate was playing up. He urgently needed to pee. 'I think we should pause now, gentlemen. My client needs a comfort break.' This had turned into something much nastier than a straightforward bigamy case. Why hadn't he been properly briefed? He collected up his papers and hurried out.

* * *

Braxton Tower had been built in the 1960s as a solution to high-density urban living, but over the years, it had become unpopular due to lack of proper maintenance and the influx of antisocial tenants. It gave an impression not of the intended 'streets in the sky' but of a bleak, savage concrete dystopia.

Sharon Vincent's high-rise flat was fifteen storeys up. Although he was pretty fit, DC Jeff Nosworthy was relieved to find that the lift was working. Once the doors closed, though, he wished he'd taken the stairs. His nostrils were assaulted by the stink of urine, stale curry and a pile of dirty nappies dumped in the corner. The lift was slow and clanked its way stoically upwards, threatening to grind to a halt at any moment. He wondered if he could hold his breath until the doors finally opened.

He had to knock several times before Sharon opened her door. She had been unable to hear above the din of her screaming children. It seemed, from their language, that Brad and Chelsey were reluctant to get dressed and go to school. Jeff doubted that he had known words like that at their age.

He pulled out his warrant card. 'Mrs Sharon Vincent? I'm Detective Constable Nosworthy from Brightsea CID. I wonder if I might have a few words.'

His background notes said she was thirty-one, but she looked at least ten years older. Her purple-streaked hair was tied up in a messy bun and she was wearing grubby ripped jeans and a hoodie. 'I've been expecting a visit from you lot.' She stood back to let him in. 'It's about Tony, isn't it? I told him the filth would catch up with him one day. No offence.' She took him into the untidy lounge and swept some junk off a chair so he could sit down. 'Fag?' She pulled a packet from the pocket of her hoodie and offered it.

'No thanks, I don't smoke.'

'Suit yourself.' She lit up and inhaled deeply.

The two children burst out of the bedroom, demanding snacks. They looked at Noz with suspicion. 'Is he a pig?'

Sharon cursed. 'Belt up, you little buggers. Go outside and play.'

'No. We want to play on the Xbox!' Noz had noticed the expensive console in the corner and the massive TV, almost covering an entire wall.

Sharon saw him looking. 'They wasn't nicked, before you ask. They're presents from a gentleman friend.' She opened the door, grabbed the kids and chucked them out. They protested vociferously, calling her an ugly old bitch, loud enough for most of the landing to hear.

'When did you last see your husband, Mrs Vincent?' Noz began to write. He needed her to sign a statement.

'He buggered off and left me when he joined that bloody band. No money for the kids, no Christmas presents, nothing. He wouldn't have married me in the first place if I hadn't been pregnant, and my brothers threatened to break his legs if he didn't.'

'I see.' Noz was trying not to be judgemental, but to his mind, this was no way to live and bring up children.

'Last I heard, he'd gone to the States with the band and I lost track of him altogether. That's until I saw his face plastered all over my celebrity magazines. He was calling himself Count Antonio Something-or-other and pretending to be Italian, but it was him all right. All done up in a posh suit and getting married to an American heiress in California, while me and the kids are living off benefits in this dump. Well, I wasn't standing for that, was I?'

'What did you do, Mrs Vincent?'

'The magazine said they were starting their honeymoon in the Now to Zen in Brightsea, so I rang reception and said I was a relative and I wanted to congratulate him on his marriage. I asked if they had his mobile number and the girl gave it to me off the computer.'

Noz reckoned that would have been against company policy, but since Meredith had been arrested, there had been a succession of temporary girls on the desk, unaware of the privacy rules. 'Did you ask him for money?'

'What do you think? I didn't ask him if he was enjoying his honeymoon, did I? I told him if he didn't cough up, I'd tell his "wife" that he was still married to me. Then you lot found out and arrested him before I could get anything out of him. Will he get put inside? Can I claim some kind of compensation?'

'I couldn't say, madam. That will be down to the court.'

Now was the time to ask her about Della Clayton.

She forestalled him. 'I heard about Della. It was all over the news. Did Tony have anything to do with it?'

Noz avoided answering that question. 'Why would you think that? Did you know her?'

'Yeah, she lived in the flat next door for a while. She was American. She told me she'd had a baby when she was very young and gave it up for adoption.' Brad and Chelsey started banging on the door, demanding to be let in. 'I sometimes wish I'd done the same.' She went across, opened the door and told them to sod off if they didn't want a clout. She lit another cigarette. 'D'you want tea or coffee or something?'

'No, I'm fine, thanks.' Noz thought it would be asking for a dose of the trots to eat or drink anything here. He could see the state of the kitchen from where he was sitting.

'I won't either. They say too much caffeine's bad for you.' She poured herself a large vodka and continued. 'After the baby, Della came over here for a fresh start and got a job as a hostess in a nightclub. That was where she met Eddie Clayton. She married him, the silly cow. He got her on the game and into cocaine.'

'Where did she go after that?'

'Dunno. She left here owing a shedload of rent, I know that much. Next thing I heard, she'd been found dead, in that same posh spa that Tony was staying in. Electrocuted, it said on the news. The word on the landing was that Eddie killed her. Then they found him dead, too. A gangland execution, they said.'

Noz could see that bad news spread incredibly fast in this environment. He had written everything down and handed the statement to her.

She glanced at it. 'From what Della told me about Eddie, I doubt if he'd have known how to electrocute somebody. He wasn't smart enough.' She signed the statement without reading it. 'Tony was, though.'

CHAPTER TWENTY-FOUR

Timothy Bennett pulled up in front of the Now to Zen Hotel and Spa with a great deal of trepidation. He'd swapped his car for a different one that he'd borrowed from the forecourt of the dealership where he'd once worked. He suspected he was being followed. It might be the police looking for him, but then again, it might not. He wasn't prepared to risk it.

A great deal had happened since he'd been abducted by the men he now thought of as 'the mob'. He'd gone into hiding, convinced they'd come after him because of what he'd seen. He'd done everything he could to change his appearance — shaved off his beard and moustache and bleached his black hair a startling brassy blonde. The suit he usually wore was replaced by jeans and a hooded jacket, and his polished shoes had morphed into trainers. Now he was risking his life returning to the place where it had all kicked off.

He had to protect Miriam and take her away to the bolthole he'd found. That's if she'd go with him. He had to convince her that she was in danger, too. This gang was ruthless enough to use her to get at him. He pulled the hood of his jacket well down over his head and approached the doorman. There was only a handful of them left now. As the hotel had fallen rapidly into decline, many of the staff had bailed out to find employment elsewhere.

Tim kept his head down as he muttered, 'I'm a guest. My wife and I are staying here. She's inside waiting for me.'

If the security guard was suspicious, he didn't show it, and stood back to let Tim through. It wasn't his problem any longer. The contract the security firm had with the Now to Zen consortium finished at the end of the week and he would be out of here. His next job was patrolling a shopping mall in the centre of town — a bit less nerve-wracking than the recent events here. First, they'd found that dead woman in the whirlpool room, and he had had to admit to discovering the place where she'd hidden after she'd slipped past him at ten thirty that night. There was a cupboard on the ground floor where they kept the little-used stuff like Christmas decorations. He'd gone there for a quiet smoke and found an empty gin bottle and the remains of some white powder. He'd tasted it to see if it was what he suspected. It was the old devil's dandruff all right — cocaine. He hadn't said anything at the time, thinking it might belong to another member of staff and he wasn't about to grass on anyone. Later, when the cops began asking questions, he'd told them about it. He'd had to make a statement.

Shortly afterwards, that nerdy bloke fell off the roof and Sir Marcus, one of the aristocracy, turned out to be a criminal and had been found mutilated in a skip. Now the cops had arrested that poncy Italian count. Time he was out of here. A bit of shoplifting would be child's play compared to what had been happening in this 'oasis of calm and tranquillity'.

* * *

Bugsy was in the lobby lounge updating an anxious Miriam on the progress of her husband's MISPER report when Tim slunk in, trying not to be conspicuous. Despite his attempts to disguise himself, Miriam recognized him immediately.

'Timsy, my darling, where have you been? I've been so worried. I'm sorry I didn't believe you. I know, now, that you really were kidnapped by thugs. I thought I'd never see you again.'

Tim ran to her. 'Oh, Mimsy, it was terrifying. I was so scared, I wet my trousers.'

Miriam grasped his bleached head and buried it in her bosom. 'My poor baby. You're safe now. Mimsy's got you.' She cradled him in her arms and rocked him.

Reluctant though he was to interrupt this touching, if somewhat astonishing, marital reunion — given their hitherto ambivalent relationship — Bugsy urgently needed to speak to Timothy Bennett. At the same time, he was aware that he was needed back at the station to resume the Vincent interview with Jack. 'Let's go into the bar, Mr Bennett. I'll buy you a drink while we talk. You look like you could use one.'

Feeling more relaxed, now that he was back with Miriam and they both had the support of a police officer, Tim recounted his story in some detail.

'You seem to have an exceptionally good recollection of the ordeal, sir.'

Tim knocked back a restorative whisky. 'I have total recall, officer. It's as if it only happened a few hours ago.'

'He's always had a photographic memory, Sergeant,' confirmed Miriam. 'It comes in very useful, sometimes.'

It could be invaluable in this case, thought Bugsy. 'Would you be able to remember the journey to the warehouse they took you to?'

'Absolutely. I can remember every set of traffic lights, every roundabout, every turning off the main road.' He grimaced. 'I wasn't planning on going back there anytime soon, though.'

'Can you remember seeing anything inside the warehouse — apart from the thugs?'

'I could see it had once been a car factory, an assembly plant. There were still engineering parts lying about. And there were stacks of military-style wooden crates in one corner. They were broken open and I could see rifles inside, AK-74Ms at a guess. Imported from Russia — there was Cyrillic writing on the outside.'

'This is very helpful, Mr Bennett. You're doing really well.' Bugsy needed to get all this information to Charlie. Bennett obviously didn't want to take them back there, but he might be persuaded with a hefty police escort and the promise of a new life for him and Miriam afterwards. 'Anything else?'

'Drugs. Thousands of pounds' worth, I'd say. The street value is probably a whole lot more. Filthy stuff.' Tim clung to Miriam and she ran her fingers through his bizarre yellow hair. She'd soon have it back to normal.

What Bugsy really wanted was to get the identity of the OCG boss. Charlie and the NCA suspected he was a high-ranking police officer. With any luck, if they found the disused factory, it would be full of prints and DNA from the two rival gangs, but they needed to cut the head off the Hydra. Given the nature of OCGs — and Hydras — no doubt two more heads would grow in its place, but it would be a start.

'Do you think you could do an e-fit of the gang leader?'

'Definitely. I'll never forget his face. Particularly when he was telling his thugs to take me away and kill me.'

'Could you describe the car he got away in?'

'Certainly. It was a Bentley. I can give you the registration number.'

Bugsy could have kissed him. If he gave this information to Charlie, maybe it would compensate slightly for having let the bastards escape with Clayton and the money.

* * *

Tony Vincent had new representation. The original duty solicitor had claimed his prostate was causing problems that prevented him from providing the legal representation that his client clearly needed. In reality, he was looking for easy cases to take him through the last six months of his working life. Murder did not come into that category, especially one as complex as this.

The new solicitor, Mrs Davenport, was a pragmatic, very experienced lady. Having been parachuted in at this late stage, she'd stayed up most of the night studying all the facts of the case. Consequently, she had no illusions about Vincent's guilt and the virtual certainty of his sentence. It was unusual for her to form any personal opinions about a client's character, but this man, she'd decided, was beyond contempt. She sat along-side him in the interview room while they waited for DI Dawes and DS Malone. DC Nosworthy, relieved to be back from the ghastly Braxton Tower and his interview with Vincent's wife, stood silently out of earshot guarding the door.

'Mr Vincent, if you'll take my advice, and I strongly recommend that you do, you'll indicate that you intend to plead guilty to the murder of Della Clayton.'

'What?' Tony obviously wasn't impressed. 'I thought you were here to get me off! What d'yer mean, cough to the murder? They'll put me away for life.'

'I fear that's inevitable, given the evidence the police now have. However, if you indicate a guilty plea at the first available opportunity — such as your appearance at the mag-istrates' court — it's possible you could receive a one-third reduction in the sentence which would otherwise be imposed, if you were found guilty at your trial. Do you understand?'

'No, I don't! Even with a third off, I'll still be inside for a bloody long time. And anyway, what bloody evidence? They ain't got nuffink that'll stand up in court. I know my rights. You need to get me a good brief.'

Mrs Davenport eyeballed him. What she really wanted to do was grasp the little shit by the front of his police-issue suit, drag him to his feet and headbutt him, but she guessed the Law Society might construe that as unprofessional. 'Listen to me very carefully, Mr Vincent. This is what the police know and can prove. Your wife — your real wife, Sharon — has confirmed Della Clayton knew you from when she lived in the flat next door, in Braxton Tower. Della recognized you from the photographs of your bigamous marriage to Abigail Jefferson in the society magazines — media coverage, I might add, which contributed massively to your eventual exposure and arrest. She contacted you, using a cheap burner phone, which a witness saw you carrying away from the pool room shortly after the murder, together with a screwdriver. Both items have since been recovered from where they were hidden in a potted palm in your hotel suite. Having been foolish enough to remove whatever gloves you wore to tamper with the wires, the items bear your fingerprints and police digital forensics have recovered the incriminating conversations between you and Della.'

Vincent recovered a piece of chewing gum he had left stuck to the underside of the table. He shoved it into his mouth and began chewing, vigorously, but said nothing.

'They know you are used to working with electrics,' she continued, 'so you had the skills to tamper with the underwater lighting in the pool, where you had arranged to meet Della. She was threatening to expose you, presumably demanding money in return for her silence. It would have meant the end of the wonderful new life you had acquired for yourself — so you killed her. That's right, isn't it?'

Despite his obvious arrogance and innate stupidity, it seemed she was getting through to him. Vincent could see it looked bad. Maybe this solicitor tart was right. She reminded him of his mother, although he hadn't seen her for years. He reckoned his best defence was to say he did it, but claim it was to save Abbie from the terrible heartache and pain of losing him. 'You're almost right, but it wasn't money Della wanted. She said she was expecting a big handout later that night from her husband, Eddie. It was Sharon who was blackmailing me for cash. Della wanted something else.'

'You'd better tell me what that was — and lose the gum, it makes you look bovine and it's extremely irritating. Added to which, it's a bad habit for a villain. The police can extract DNA from chewing gum.'

CHAPTER TWENTY-FIVE

Officers from the National Crime Agency turned out in force to accompany Timothy Bennett, who had reluctantly agreed to take them back to the warehouse.

Afterwards, Charlie updated Bugsy on the progress. 'Obviously we didn't expect the guns and drugs to be there, but you'd be surprised at the amount of evidence that was left behind, including Eddie Clayton's fingers, scattered on the floor.'

'I don't suppose the OCG expected Bennett to be able to locate their hideout from the one brief and harrowing visit during the night,' Bugsy observed.

'The man has astounding recall,' agreed Charlie. 'Thanks to him, we harvested a good deal of DNA and fingerprints from gang members, including the identity of the head of the OCG. We're about to pick him up. He's going to get one hell of a shock. We certainly did, when we found out who he was.'

* * *

The entire family had turned out to celebrate Sir Reginald Cribbs's sixtieth birthday. He could easily have passed for ten years younger, were it not for the slight paunch where a flat belly used to be, and the touch of distinguished silver at his temples. Everyone was out in the garden, enjoying the sun. The super-mansion, set in two acres of land, afforded Sir Reginald the privacy and security that was so essential in his line of business. Guests were sipping chilled rosé and nibbling sausages, steaks and burgers from the barbecue. Reggie — full of bonhomie and wearing an apron and a paper crown, proclaiming him 'King of the BBQ' — wielded tongs and a long-handled fork. There was music, merriment and birthday congratulations as he handed out the food. To a casual observer, he was the epitome of a caring, loving family man enjoying an afternoon in the bosom of his caring, loving family.

The grandchildren besieged him, grabbing his hands and dragging him away. 'Come on, Gramps. Come and play cricket with us.'

Which is what he was doing when the NCA officers arrived. The security guard had let the unmarked police cars through the locked gates, assuming they were more of Sir Reginald's extensive family here for the party. The house-keeper directed them to the lawns at the back of the house, where Sir Reggie had just been bowled out for a duck.

If Cribbs was shocked, he concealed it well. He was ami-able and cooperative when the officers took him to one side and showed him the warrant to search his house.

'We need you to come with us to answer some ques-tions about your businesses, Sir Reginald. We have irrefuta-ble evidence that you are involved in illicit activities relating to organized crime.'

He laughed. 'That's absolutely ridiculous. All my busi-nesses are perfectly legal. I deal in the import and export of chemicals and fertilizers.' He glanced around him. Several of the party guests, including his sons, were watching, con-cerned. 'Could we discuss this inside, officers? I'm sure we can clear up any misunderstanding very quickly. Then per-haps you'd like to join us for some food and wine?' He led the way towards the house. His wife saw him leaving and called after him.

'Reggie, is everything all right?'

'Absolutely fine, darling. This won't take long.'

And it didn't. As soon as they entered the hall, Cribbs dashed to an unlocked gun cabinet, grabbed an AK-74 rifle and pointed it at the officers. 'Back off or I'll fire.'

They were in no doubt that he meant it and drew back, with their hands up. Still pointing the rifle, he made for the side door into the drive, where his car was parked. 'No sudden moves,' he yelled.

He slammed the door shut behind him and ran for it with the NCA officers in hot pursuit. He yanked open the car door, then turned and opened fire. He managed to wing one of the officers before two others pulled handguns. It was a crack-shot female officer who took him out, with a perfectly placed bullet to the chest.

* * *

'Was he a top-brass copper, like you suspected?' Bugsy was getting all the guff from Charlie while eating a jam doughnut, his first since he wound up in hospital. The jam had dripped down his chin and onto his tie without him even noticing.

'No, not at all. Ostensibly, Sir Reginald Cribbs was a successful and respected businessman, living with his wife in a multi-million-pound property near Hampstead Heath. Not only that, but he was on the board of trustees of a police charity and a member of several independent advisory groups working with the police to improve services.'

'Blimey,' said Bugsy. 'It was a bloody good cover. Somehow, you don't expect these hoodlums to have a background of propriety, let alone a knighthood.'

'That's how they avoid capture for so long. In the NCA, we've learned not to believe anything we hear and only half of what we actually witness with our own eyes. Racketeers don't all go about behaving like the Krays anymore.'

'What happens to Cribbs's ill-gotten gains?' Bugsy wondered.

'The house is in his wife's name, as you would expect. She'll have a good lawyer, so the chances of proving she knew what his business was really about are pretty much zero. He owns — or should I say owned — the Bentley and several other top-of-the-range vehicles, all of which have been confiscated, along with a good deal of money we found under the floor of his summer house. This has been a vitally useful operation, Bugsy. In addition to recovering guns, drugs and cash, the NCA boffins have been able to access and eliminate an encrypted communications platform, being used for purely criminal purposes by countless crooks in the UK alone.'

'That's good news, Charlie. I know you'd have nicked him, whoever he was, but I'm glad he wasn't a copper. You wouldn't believe how angry the MIT was when Jack was wrongly accused of corruption. You don't ever want to believe that one of your own has gone rogue.' Bugsy frowned. 'What did Cribbs hope to gain by opening fire? He must have known the NCA officers would be armed.'

'I think it was a "shit or bust" moment. He'd guessed we'd turned over his warehouse and we'd soon have done the same to his house. The evidence of corruption and murders would nail him for life. The only way out was to run for it. Goodness knows what he planned to do after that. I suppose he didn't want to spend what time he had left banged up. In any event, it didn't half put a dampener on his birthday party.'

Bugsy grinned. 'I bet it did. We must have a drink to celebrate, but right now I'm still involved in questioning the man suspected of murdering Eddie "Coke" Clayton's missus.' He paused. 'What'll happen to Tim Bennett? Even though Cribbs is dead, I expect there are still criminals out there who won't want him to testify.'

'The Witness Protection unit has moved Mr and Mrs Bennett to a safe house. After Mr Bennett testifies, they'll be put on a plane to Spain with different identities. They plan to run a beach bar together — *La Chiringuito de Tim y Mim*. As Mrs Bennett jokingly pointed out, "Tim spends most of his time in a pub so I might as well join him. That way, I can see what he's up to and keep him out of trouble." They seem to be genuinely devoted to each other. I think they'll make a success of it.'

Bugsy reflected that the dreadful events of their recent past had reminded the Bennetts how much they meant to each other. At least some good had come of it.

* * *

Back in the Brightsea station interview room, Jack and Bugsy joined Tony Vincent with Mrs Davenport riding shotgun. Noz turned on the digital recorder and Davenport identified herself.

'Eleanor Davenport, duty solicitor, representing Tony Leyton Orient Vincent.'

Blimey, thought Bugsy. *No wonder Tony never mentioned his middle names. His dad was obviously a supporter of the O's. I wonder if Vincent's alter ego would have called himself Count Antonio Juventus AC Milan Di Vincenzo.*

Mrs Davenport continued. 'My client wishes to change his statement, DI Dawes. He is ready to confess to the murder of Della Clayton, and in his defence, he believes there are extenuating circumstances. He wishes them to be taken into consideration now, and later, when he will rely on them in court.'

This should be good, thought Bugsy. *What possible mitigating circumstances could the bloke have for a premeditated murder designed to shut someone up?*

The room went quiet, apart from the squelching sound of Vincent's chewing. After a few long seconds, with no one saying anything, his solicitor glared at him. 'Mr Vincent? Your statement for the tape?'

'Oh, yeah. You want me to tell them what occurred. OK.' He spat the gum into his hand and stuck it to the underside of the table. 'Well, it was like this. She — Della, that is — used to live in the flat next door to me and Sharon in Braxton Tower. Proper dump, it was.'

It still is, agreed Noz, silently. *And your kids are running wild there.*

'Anyway, she recognized me from the photos of my superstar wedding of the year to Abbie. The magazines said we were starting our honeymoon in one of her dad's posh spa hotels in Brightsea. Well, Della got hold of my mobile number somehow — I'm guessing she conned it from one of the staff — and said she wanted to talk to me about something important. She threatened to expose me if I didn't agree to meet her. Well, I couldn't let her give me away, could I? After all, this was my mega-minted future we were talking about. Hot, big-ticket cars, private planes, luxury yachts and all that stuff. I had to keep my eyes on the prize. Though I say it myself, I did a bloody good job at being Count Antonio Di Vincenzo. I wasn't about to throw it all away on the say-so of some old bag from my past.' He paused, casting his mind back. 'I'd been in one of those twilight whirlpools with Abbie, and I remember thinking at the time that the underwater lights could be a bit moody, especially if the wires were crossed. It was then I got the idea.'

'What time did you arrange the meeting with Della?' Jack asked.

'Eleven o'clock. Abbie was asleep by ten, so it gave me time to get down there and fix the wires before Della turned up. She said eleven would be OK as she'd arranged to blag some money off her old man later on, at eleven thirty.'

That would agree with the time of her death, before Clayton got there, mused Jack. 'Did she try to "blag" some money from you, in return for her silence?'

Vincent looked at his solicitor and she nodded.

'Funnily enough, no, she didn't.'

'What did she want?' asked Bugsy.

Eleanor Davenport nodded again.

'She said I had to give Abbie up. Tell her the marriage was over, then go away, somewhere abroad, and never contact her again. Well, I wasn't going to do that, was I? What kind of plonker would leave a wife who was heiress to all those millions of dollars? And anyway, what had it got to do with her, the snotty cow? She was never very fond of Sharon or the kids. Never lent her no money nor nuffink.'

Noz was sitting quietly, making notes, but Jack could see him resisting, with some difficulty, the urge to punch the creep on the chin. He kept getting flashbacks of Vincent's real wife, trapped in that seedy flat with Brad and Chelsey. With any luck, and a sensible judge, Vincent would end up trapped in an even seedier cell, but in his case, it would be for the rest of his active life. At least then he'd be safe from Noz.

'What happened next?' Jack wanted to know.

'Obviously, I told her I wasn't going to do nuffink of the sort. She said if I didn't, she'd tell Abbie about Sharon and the kids herself. We argued for a bit, then I snatched her phone off of her, so no one could trace her calls to me and I shoved her in the whirlpool.' He showed no emotion.

'Then what?' Jack spoke through clenched teeth.

'Well, the circuit shorted, the lights sparked and the pump stopped working, like you'd expect.'

'No, I mean what did you do next?'

'Oh, I see. I made sure she was dead then legged it back to the suite. I wasn't going to hang about for her old man to turn up. I thought, with any luck, he'd get the blame. You lot usually pin it on the husband, when a wife's found murdered, don't you? Easiest option. I bumped into that dopey girl, Kelly-Anne, on the stairs. I spun her a line about being a film director and giving her a part in my next film if she kept her mouth shut.' He had the gall to laugh at that. 'Well, I had to think on my feet, didn't I? I suppose she told you about the phone and the screwdriver. Big mistake on my part.'

Jack thought it was as if he was making a mental note not to be so careless next time he murdered someone. This bloke really was a piece of work. 'Mrs Davenport mentioned that you believe you have extenuating circumstances — some sort of mitigation for what you did.'

'Yeah, that's right.' He straightened his shoulders and adopted a more articulate tone, as if rehearsing how he would say his next words in court. 'I did it to protect Abbie's mental health. She's passionately in love with me. It would have broken her heart if I'd dumped her. She'd have gone to pieces. Might even have committed suicide. I didn't want that on my conscience, did I? I had to kill Della — I had no choice. I mean, she should have minded her own business, shouldn't she?' He looked around him, expecting nods of empathy. There weren't any.

Jack stood up. 'Miss Jefferson is going to have to manage without you now, Mr Vincent, because you're going away for a very long time. Stand up, please.' Jack formally charged him then gestured to Noz. 'DC Nosworthy, get him out of my sight.'

After he'd gone, Jack approached Eleanor Davenport, who was putting her laptop back into her briefcase. 'I can't help thinking you weren't totally convinced by your client's extenuating circumstances, Mrs Davenport.'

She smiled. 'The man's an arse. More to the point, he'll be on a hiding to nothing, if his barrister is daft enough to claim mitigation on those grounds. What jury is going to believe he was forced to commit murder because the beautiful, rich, entitled young heiress that he cheated, lied to and married bigamously might be so mortified at losing him that she'd kill herself if he left her?'

'Never mind the clout on the jaw he gave her when he was trying to escape,' added Bugsy.

Jack frowned. 'He says Della Clayton didn't ask him for money to keep quiet, like his wife Sharon did.'

'No. I thought that was a bit strange. But he's adamant she didn't demand cash. She just wanted him to leave Abbie alone.'

Jack looked puzzled. 'Why do you suppose that was?'

Eleanor shook her head. 'No idea. After twenty-five years as a solicitor, I've given up trying to work out why people do unpredictable things. Maybe Della Clayton was just one of those principled women who couldn't stand by and see Vincent's wife and children abandoned, while he lived the high life with a younger version, so she decided to put a stop to it.'

'Doubt it,' said Bugsy. 'She was a sex worker, a cocaine addict and a shoplifter. And she was married to Eddie Clayton for several years — a vicious gangster with no principles at all. There has to be more to it than that.'

* * *

The answer came in a report from Doctor Nielsen, the pathologist, and it astonished everybody. He delivered it to DI Dawes in person, suspecting there might be questions as to its reliability.

'I believe you may find this interesting, Inspector Dawes. I have also emailed it to you for your digital records.' He handed Jack the hard copy and waited while he scanned the scientific jargon.

'In the interests of my sanity, Doctor, what exactly is this telling me?'

'It's the result of nuclear deoxyribonucleic acid testing – better known as DNA. During the course of the Della Clayton murder investigation, your predecessor, DI Long, required teams of SOCOs to carry out extensive DNA sampling on virtually everyone present in the Now to Zen at the time of the murder — especially those guests who wanted to leave.'

'Yes, I remember. I gave a sample myself. She was hoping it would somehow prove I was the killer.'

'She told *me* that PACE says we can't go around demanding fingerprints and DNA from people without their consent, unless we have good reason to suspect them of having committed an offence,' complained Noz.

'I don't think she cared what PACE said, by that time,' said Bugsy. 'She was determined to present the CPS with a watertight case against Inspector Dawes.'

'Most people gave their consent just to be allowed to return home,' continued Doctor Nielsen. 'One such person was Abigail Jefferson, although her husband refused for reasons that have now become obvious.' He cleared his throat, preparing for the bombshell. 'Maternal DNA testing proves, scientifically, the biological relationship between mother and child. The results of a maternal test are unambiguous, providing a 99.99% accurate result in cases where the tested woman is the biological mother.'

'Sorry, Doc, still not with you,' said Bugsy.

'What I'm saying, Sergeant Malone, is that Della Clayton was Abigail Jefferson's birth mother.'

CHAPTER TWENTY-SIX

'What are you going to do, Jack?' Corrie was packing for the journey home. Jack was looking out of the window at the Jeffersons' private limousine in the car park.

'Me? I'm not going to do anything. As far as the police are concerned, the investigation's over. The men responsible for the murders of Eddie and Della Clayton have been apprehended and the ones still alive are awaiting their trials, where I'm confident they will receive appropriately jaw-dropping sentences. Obviously Bugsy and I will be required to give evidence, but in the meantime, I'm just looking forward to getting back to the comfort of our own home, rugby on the telly and your cooking.'

'Yes, but what about poor Abbie? She must be so sad and confused.'

'Carter and Lola Jefferson have flown over in their private jet. Their car's outside. I assume they're talking to Dick and Penny Hawkins about the future of this place, if it has one. Then they'll take Abbie home to California.'

'They'll have some explaining to do,' Corrie said.

'Wait until the media get hold of the story. One minute it's the celebrity wedding of the year, then the "mouth-wateringly handsome groom" is arrested for murder and bigamy and the "adorable bride" goes home to her mother — except it seems she isn't her mother.'

'You're such a cynic, Jack. The press won't print anything like that.'

'Don't you believe it. If there's one thing those gossip columnists like more than a glamorous, extravagant wedding between two beautiful, privileged people, it's the aftermath, when it all goes wrong. They're like sharks scenting blood. It'll be a feeding frenzy.'

There was a tap on the door. Corrie opened it and Abbie was standing there. Corrie invited her in, hoping she hadn't overheard any of their conversation. She looked smaller, somehow, and very sad.

'I've come to say goodbye. I'm going back home with Mom and Dad. Corrie, you were real kind to me after Toni hit me that time. I just wanted to say if you and Jack would come to LA for a vacation at the Now to Zen, that'd be great. You can't have enjoyed being here, after . . . well . . . after everything that's happened. Especially you, Jack.'

'None of it was your fault, Abbie,' Jack assured her.

'Are you OK, dear?' Corrie admonished herself. 'Silly question, of course you're not.'

'I feel like it's all a bad dream. My husband isn't the man I thought I'd fallen in love with — he's a cheap crook, already married to someone else, and even worse, I've just found out my mom isn't really my mom.' She took a deep, shuddering breath to avoid bursting into tears. 'Mom explained everything. Della gave birth to me in the States when she was scarcely more than a child herself. She didn't even know who my father was. Mom and Dad wanted kids but couldn't have any. Della gave me to them when I was just a few weeks old. She'd already picked out a name — Abigail, so Mom and Dad decided to stick with it. Mom said Della knew I'd have a better life with them. Then she came here to the UK and forgot all about me.'

'I don't expect she did, not for a single moment,' insisted Corrie. 'She still cared about you, didn't she? When she recognized Tony Vincent from your wedding photos in her magazine, she knew your marriage was a scam to get access to your money. She came here to tell him to leave you alone and lost her life trying to protect you.'

Abbie thought about it. 'Yeah, I guess she did.'

Jack recalled how she had also planned to get money from Eddie Clayton, so she could move back to the US. Digital forensics had found the conversation on the phone Vincent took from Della. No doubt she'd hoped that one day, she might get to know her daughter, even if it was only from a distance.

'What you need to do now,' Corrie continued, 'is go home, heal for a while, then regroup and come out fighting. Your mum and dad have loved you and looked after you all your life, so they're your real parents in everything but biology, which couldn't matter less.'

'You're right. It doesn't matter, does it?' She looked brighter.

'You'll meet someone — somebody genuine, who'll love you for who you are, not what you are,' Corrie assured her. 'Just give it time.'

Abbie smiled for the first time. 'You're a real kind lady, Corrie.' She turned towards the door. 'Don't forget what I said about a Now to Zen vacation in California.'

After she'd gone, Jack put his arms around Corrie. 'You handled that really well, sweetheart. I'm proud of you. It could have been our Carlene that you were comforting.'

Corrie disagreed. 'No, it couldn't. If any man treated our Carlene like Tony Vincent treated Abbie, my reaction would be very different.'

'Why? What would you do?'

'I'd take him into my kitchen, explain to him the error of his ways — then I'd cut off his balls with my filleting knife.'

* * *

'I've just had an email saying that the consortium is closing down the Brightsea branch of the Now to Zen Hotel and

Spa.' Richard Hawkins was putting paperwork through the shredder.

'Are you surprised?' Penny Hawkins carried on deleting files from the computer. 'One murder, two attempted murders, extensive digital fraud and keeping a disorderly house.'

'That last one's a bit harsh, Penny. It was just a few gentlemen taking advantage of some late-night treatment opportunities.'

'And you, taking advantage of the extra money,' Penny pointed out. 'Don't think I didn't see you trousering the cash.'

'In my defence,' retorted Richard, 'your precious and respectable Sir Marcus Wellbeloved turned out to be a cocaine king. We were harbouring public enemy number one.'

Penny wrinkled her nose with chagrin. 'It's easy for you to say with hindsight. How was I supposed to know? He was charming, charismatic and well-dressed.'

'So was Al Capone — allegedly. "Sir Marcus" also left without paying his bill. His credit card was a fake, like him.'

Penny picked up a brochure and studied it, then tore it in half. 'What do you think they'll do with the place?'

Richard stopped shredding. 'The site is being turned into one of Jefferson's new projects, a multi-entertainment venue, with amusement arcades and cinemas and clubs.'

Penny frowned. 'I don't think I want to work in one of those, do you?'

'Where will we go now, do you think?'

'How about Cornwall?' She turned her screen around so he could see the picture of a chocolate-box pub and an online advert. 'They're seeking "a reliable couple with experience in the hospitality sector" to run it. You can pull pints and I'll make pasties.'

He grinned. 'It's a deal. Time we left Brightsea and the Now to Zen Corporation behind.'

'We were just thinking the same,' said Jack. He and Corrie appeared at the desk, ready to check out. A porter hovered with their luggage.

'You're one of the last to leave,' said Penny. 'It's at this point that I usually ask, "Have you enjoyed your stay?" but under the circumstances . . .' She tailed off.

'Probably better if we skip that bit,' agreed Corrie. 'Well, good luck and if you want a recipe for *tiddy oggies*, let me know.'

'What the hell's a *tiddy oggie?*' muttered Jack.

Outside in the car park, Corrie spotted Louis striding with his backpack towards one of the Jefferson cars. She called out to him. 'Hey, Louis! Where are you off to, now the spa's closing?'

'Corrie, really!' Jack scolded. 'It's none of our business.'

'I know, but I just want to find out if my hunch was right.'

Louis jogged across on the balls of his feet. 'Hey, Corrie. I'm going to LA as Abbie's personal trainer. She's very down at the moment and she wants me to design a strenuous five-day workout routine to take her mind off that bastard who deceived her. What will happen to him, Jack?'

'He'll serve life, in all probability.'

'Good. He deserves everything he gets after what he put Abbie through. Hopefully, I can show her that some of us blokes are decent and genuine. She's had a bad experience, but I reckon I can help with exercise and sports psychology. She showed me a picture of her gym — it's awesome. Anyway, I'll see you guys around.' He turned to go but called back, 'Keep up with the squats and lunges, Corrie. Couple of weeks and you'll have bum cheeks like coconuts.'

After he'd gone, Jack glanced at Corrie's face. 'You've got that smug look that you always get when you've been proved right.'

Corrie watched Louis climb into the back of the limousine next to Abbie. 'I think that young man will end up being rather more than a five-day personal trainer. I'm glad. He's just what she needs.'

Jack shrugged. 'This spa is the very last place I'd consider for match-making opportunities. You'd be safer with online dating. Come on, let's go. We should be home in time to see the New Zealand versus Australia match.' He felt a tap on his shoulder.

'Hi there, Jack and Corrie. I'm Kelly-Anne, your spa buddy.' She stopped. 'Only I'm not anymore, am I?' She looked bewildered.

Corrie put an arm around her. 'I'm so sorry about you losing your spa buddy job, Kelly-Anne. You were very good at it.'

'And Vincent promising you a part in a non-existent film. That was cruel,' added Jack. 'What will you do now?'

She brightened. 'It's going to be OK. My agent has got me a spot in *The Great British Modelling Challenge.'*

'Well, now, with your beautiful figure and lovely face, that's perfect for you,' Corrie enthused.

Kelly-Anne looked puzzled. 'I don't think it matters what you look like, it's the modelling that counts.'

'How do you mean?' asked Jack. 'Won't you be modelling clothes?'

She laughed. 'No, silly! The challenge is to make an animal out of modelling clay in the shortest possible time. I've been practising. I'm going to make a snake. You just have to roll the clay into a long, thin sausage, poke holes for its eyes, then coil it up like a cobra.'

'Does it pay well?' asked Jack, thinking there was a risk her 'snake' would look more like dog poo.

'Oh yes, and they give you really pretty aprons. Well, bye-bye then, Jack and Corrie. *Arrivo la derchi.'* She tottered away, giggling, on her impossibly high wedges.

'What did you make of that?' asked Corrie.

Jack shook his head. 'I'm lost for words. Is that what passes for entertainment these days?'

'Compared to most reality game shows, that one sounds quite intellectual.'

'Let's go home.'

* * *

They were cruising slowly along the Brightsea promenade in a tailback of holiday traffic when Corrie spotted something.

'Look over there, Jack. It's a mobile police station.' The white van with the familiar blue-and-yellow Battenburg markings was parked in a lay-by on the opposite side of the road, circled by traffic cones.

Jack glanced at it. 'It's a police information van,' he said. 'They'll be notifying the public about the new driving laws, like phone penalties and smart motorways. I don't know who's manning it, but it must be the most boring police job in the world. Imagine Joe Public coming in every day and asking daft questions about clean air zones and speed limiters. I expect it's some copper working out his time before retiring.'

'No, it isn't.' Corrie grinned. 'I just saw Inspector Lorraine Long "assisting" a member of the public out of the van with his arm up his back. He obviously didn't ask the right questions.'

'Blimey!' said Jack. 'I'm not laughing — really I'm not.'

CHAPTER TWENTY-SEVEN

David discharged himself against the advice of the private Carter Jefferson clinic. He was on crutches and brimming with meds, but felt he was able to function without full-time nursing support. He was anxious to go home to his bedsit and some semblance of normality. His recent experience had nightmarish qualities that he'd never previously encountered in the safe, digital world of software. He had no wish to repeat them. On a more practical level, there wouldn't be any food in his fridge. He didn't want to attract the unwanted attention of his mother — she'd only make a fuss. So far, he'd managed to avoid telling her exactly what had happened to him, just that he was away on business. He decided to call a taxi and get the driver to stop off at the nearest supermarket, so he could buy a few items to tide him over. Once outside in the fresh air, he took a couple of deep breaths to brace himself, but now he was unsure whether he was strong enough for such an undertaking.

'David? How are you feeling?' Rainbow was there, waiting for him. She'd been visiting regularly and left instructions with the clinic to let her know as soon as he came out.

David was pitifully pleased to see her. Tears stung his eyes and he realized that he was still very weak. 'Hello, Rainbow. I'm much better, thank you.'

She took his bag with his personal items and the medication he needed and steered him gently towards her car. 'I'm taking you home to my flat. The doctors said that you should never have left the hospital, let alone try to go back to a bedsit. You'll need support until you're well enough to cope on your own.'

For a few wonderful moments, a huge wave of relief engulfed him before common sense kicked in. 'That's really kind, but you don't have to do that. I'll manage.'

'No, you won't. I could see, as soon as you appeared at the door, there's a blockage in the fourth astral layer of your aura. It signifies stagnated energy. The fourth layer is vitally important to your overall health, considering its attachment to the heart chakra. I can help you learn to keep it in balance.'

David surrendered gratefully. 'I'm so happy to see you, Rainbow. Are you sure I won't be in the way?'

She took his arm. 'Of course not. I don't have a job anymore. They've closed down the Brightsea Now to Zen. I'll ask for a transfer to another of their spas, but in the meantime, you're my priority.'

David had no idea where his 'heart chakra' was, but he could have sworn he felt it leap as she put her arms around him to guide him into the car. Now wasn't the time to discuss it, but the Jefferson US IT manager had been in touch. He'd congratulated David on a job well done, commiserated with his injuries and the danger he'd put himself in on behalf of the company. He had then offered him promotion and a huge increase in salary. The only problem, and now it didn't seem like a problem at all, was that the job would mean moving to the Jefferson IT headquarters in LA. His mother would have a fit, but she'd get used to it. She had her charities and committees and her bridge parties — and she could visit him, for holidays. Leaving Rainbow, on the other hand, was an entirely different prospect. He looked across at her, thinking her name suited her perfectly. He couldn't read auras but if he had been able to, he thought hers would be bright with the colours of love, joy and happiness. He'd spent too much of his life missing opportunities because of his crippling shyness. He wasn't going to miss this one.

'Rainbow, do you think you might apply for a transfer to the flagship Now to Zen Hotel and Spa, in California?'

She smiled. 'Is that where you're going?'

'Yes. I've been offered a job there.'

'Then of course I shall.'

* * *

The Withenshaw family was out in force to welcome Fred and Rita back to their cosy semi-detached home on the corner of Ribble Street. As the taxi pulled up outside, there were cheers from the little crowd waiting in the front garden. Due to Rita's lack of modern communication devices, they had little or no idea of how the holiday had gone. Rita had searched for postcards, but apparently people didn't send them anymore.

'Did you have a good time, Mam and Dad?' asked their eldest daughter, who had been primarily responsible for arranging everything. 'Was it relaxing?'

'Oh aye,' said Fred. 'First night we got there, there was a murder — some lass was electrocuted by the lights in the whirlpool. Then a young fella got pushed off the roof and all but snuffed it. A copper — a detective inspector — got himself arrested because he had a dodgy gun, but it was a mistake. We found out later that another guest, a smartly dressed chap, was a real gangster. He was kidnapped, tortured and shot by the mob that he'd double-crossed.'

Rita put a mug of strong, sweet tea in Fred's hand, hoping to shut him up. He paused to take a noisy but satisfying slurp, then ploughed on, undaunted.

'The daughter of Carter Jefferson, the hotel owner — filthy rich, mind — was honeymooning in the suite above us. Her new Italian hubby, Count Antonio Something-or-other, turned out to be a cockney bigamist, and they found out that it was him who'd killed the first lass in the twilight pool. He ran into the sea to escape, but they caught him and took him away in handcuffs. Other than that, it was quite restful, wasn't it, Mother?'

The family looked seriously alarmed. 'Mam, is any of that true?'

Rita laughed and gave Fred a playful but telling punch on the arm. 'No, of course it isn't. Take no notice of your dad. He's been watching too many of those murder mysteries on the telly. We had a lovely time. The food was excellent and very refined.'

'Aye,' agreed Fred. 'I had haddock, chips and mushy peas, three nights in a row. Real tasty, it were. Happen I'll just go up and soak me feet while you cook t'tea, Mother.' He went out into the hall and there was an expectant pause and giggling among the family.

'He's going to say it,' whispered one of the grandkids.

'He always says it,' confirmed another.

'Well, I'll go to t'foot of our stairs!' Fred came back in. 'Come and see, Mother. We've got one of those chairs that go up t'staircase.'

'We had to get you both out of the way while they put it in,' said their daughter. 'It's the rest of your anniversary present. We hope you like it.'

'It's wonderful, love. Thank you all so very much. This has been an anniversary we'll never forget, hasn't it, Dad?'

'Aye, it has that.'

* * *

It was happy hour in the Garwood household and Cynthia was mixing gin cocktails for herself and George. She always thought there was something uplifting about the chink of the ice cubes as she dropped them into the glass. She was slicing limes when she heard the phone ring. They were obliged, George said, to maintain a landline for police contact purposes. She rarely used it, preferring her mobile, but he liked it. Being a little hard of hearing, he could turn up the speaker.

She had assured him he could do the same with his smartphone, but he'd never quite grasped it, no matter how many times she'd shown him. Although she was in the room next to his study, she could hear the conversation clearly.

'Detective Chief Superintendent Garwood here.' Cynthia always thought it was a pompous way to answer the phone, especially when you didn't know who was calling. What was wrong with 'Hello'?

'Garwood, this is Sir Barnaby. I'm ringing to talk to you about DI Dawes. In particular, his involvement in the recent incidents at the Now to Zen Hotel and Spa in Brightsea, especially the murder.'

Cynthia peered through the crack in the door. She grinned as George surreptitiously put down the *Echo* and stood to attention. He pulled his shoulders back, straightened his tie and braced himself for what he suspected was coming.

'Ah. Yes, sir. Bad business — very bad. Dawes is something of an iconoclast, I'm afraid. Of course, I should point out that he and his wife were on holiday at the time, so not officially under my command.'

'So you weren't responsible for him taking over as SIO?'

George blustered, trying desperately to avoid what was shaping up to be a very damaging attack on his judgement. 'Er . . . only indirectly, sir. Hardly at all, in fact. The chief superintendent at Brightsea notified me that the IPOC wanted the murder investigation reopened. He argued that as Dawes was on the spot and had had close involvement in the case, he was best placed to take charge. Naturally, I was very unhappy about it, sir. It hadn't been too long since Dawes himself had been a suspect. However, against my better judgement, I gave him authority to take over.' He took a deep breath, waiting for Sir Barnaby's reaction.

'I see.' There was a pause that went on for a long, anxious moment. Garwood took it to mean he was off the hook. Then Sir Barnaby continued, 'Well, I thought you should know that I've had a call from the deputy chief constable of the Brightsea constabulary, thanking me for DI Dawes's invaluable input, culminating in the arrest of a dangerous murderer. He also commended DS Malone's brave attempt at apprehending a County Lines drug dealer and obtaining valuable information, enabling the NCA to dismantle an organized crime group.' *The head of which*, he thought ruefully, *I had believed to be a good friend*. 'I was actually ringing to congratulate you on an inspired decision to put Dawes and Malone in there, Garwood, but it appears it's inappropriate.'

Garwood backtracked hastily. 'Well, obviously I was able to see that Dawes and Malone would make a far better job of investigation than the woman Brightsea had put in charge.'

The commander choked, audibly. 'I do hope, Garwood, that you're not implying DI Long was incompetent because she's a woman. The modern police service is fully committed to eliminating unlawful and unfair discrimination, promoting equality and diversity and protecting human rights.'

'Absolutely, sir.' Garwood was starting to sweat. He could feel it running down inside his collar. 'I agree, wholeheartedly. I'll pass on your generous comments to Dawes and Malone. Thank you for ringing, sir. Have a good evening, sir. Goodbye, sir.'

Garwood tottered into the drawing room. He snatched both gin cocktails from Cynthia's hands. 'Gimme those,' he gasped. 'I need a drink! I need two!'

* * *

When Jack returned to Kings Richington police station, there were loud cheers. As he walked through the MIT incident room, there was a round of applause from the team.

He put a package down on the desk. 'There you go, folks. A dozen sticks of Brightsea rock — souvenirs from the worst holiday I've ever spent. I'm so glad to be back.'

'It's good to have you back, sir.' Gemma went as far as to kiss him on the cheek, then stepped back, blushing.

'The sarge has filled us in on everything that's happened,' said Aled. 'Crackin' job, sir.'

'Hard to believe all that corruption could happen in a little seaside resort like Brightsea.' Mitch had worked in London for most of his career and thought all the real crime happened there. Now it seemed that some of the worst of it was seeping into the suburbs.

'That's what you get when you skive off on holiday,' said Sergeant Parsloe, shaking Jack's hand.

Bugsy went so far as to give Jack a man hug. 'You only had 'em worried for a few minutes, guv. I told 'em we'd soon get it sorted.'

Gemma was still outraged. 'I can't believe that DI Long really thought she could get away with charging you with murder and corruption. Calls herself a detective?'

'She had no chance,' grinned Jack. 'Not with you guys on my side.' *And the Three Cs*, he thought ruefully. 'DC Nosworthy deserves some credit, too.'

'Except he isn't a DC anymore,' said Bugsy. 'I've heard he's been promoted to DS for his part in catching the real killer in the Della Clayton case.'

'Well deserved,' said Jack. 'It isn't always right to blindly follow the orders of your detective inspector, when your instinct tells you it's wrong.'

'I'll remember that, sir, when you haul me over the coals for using my initiative,' said Aled.

'Like the time you broke into the convent of St Columbanus without backup and nearly got sacrificed on a tombstone,' said Gemma, with a scathing look in her eye. 'That was really showing initiative.'

DC Williams was attempting to ping a rubber band at DC Fox, when the door opened and Chief Superintendent Garwood strode in. He approached Jack and patted him on the back.

'Congratulations, DI Dawes. You did an excellent job. You too, Malone. Sir Barnaby was very complimentary about my decision to put you in charge of the Clayton investigation.

Obviously, I never had any doubts about your integrity and your ability to catch the murderer. I told Sir Barnaby that I'd had total confidence in you right from the start.'

The team, now silent, exchanged glances of pure disbelief. This was the man who not so very long ago was forbidding them to make any inquiries of their own to prove Jack's innocence. He'd gone as far as to threaten them with Reg 15 disciplinary notices.

Incensed at this blatant hypocrisy, Gemma was unable to stay silent. 'Sorry, sir, but didn't you tell us there was strong evidence linking the DI to police corruption and that you were looking to assign his replacement?'

There were noises around the room which, if Garwood hadn't known better, could have been the early rumblings of a mutiny.

'I don't remember saying anything of the sort, DC Fox. I think your recollection is badly flawed.'

Bugsy offered Garwood a stick of Brightsea rock in an upward gesture that might have been construed as vaguely obscene.

He strode hastily towards the door, anxious to return to the sanctuary of his office and Nancy, who would make him a cup of strong coffee. 'Anyway — well done. Er . . . carry on, everyone.'

EPILOGUE

It was a warm, pleasant Saturday evening. Jack and Corrie were sitting outside on the patio, enjoying a glass of wine. He was reading the sports page of the *Richington Echo*, and she was scrolling through her menu files, trying to decide on a suitable five-course dinner for the Kings Richington Rugby Club's annual bash. *Nothing fancy*, she'd been told, *just some fodder to fill the gap between drinks at the bar, the speeches, the stripper and more drinks at the bar.*

Corrie finally broke the silence. 'OK, go ahead and say it.'

Jack looked up. 'Say what?'

'"I told you so." That's what you were thinking, wasn't it?'

'No, it wasn't,' said Jack, affronted. 'I was thinking that the Richington Renegades won't win next Saturday's match unless they beef up the front row.'

'I bet you weren't,' accused Corrie. 'I bet you were thinking that the last time we were sitting here like this, I booked us a holiday at the Brightsea Now to Zen and you didn't want to go — but I ignored you.'

Jack answered from behind his newspaper. It was safer. 'Sweetheart, I wouldn't be churlish enough to remind you that it was your idea to have a relaxing break, submerged in an oasis of pampering. You know — the one where I got thrown in the slammer by the detective from hell, and you, Cynthia and Carlene morphed into the Miss Marple triplets.'

Corrie pulled a face. 'It wasn't all bad. Didn't you say Bugsy has been put forward for a commendation for bravery, above and beyond the call of duty?'

'Yep. He's a bloody good copper. He deserves it. There's nobody I'd rather have watching my back.'

'Iris says she still can't give him a hug without his ribs hurting. Dr Griffin reckons there were at least two broken in the attack. He must have been in a lot of pain.'

'The officers from the NCA got the thugs who did it. They rounded up the whole OCG after the head honcho was shot. There's a rumour going round that he was a chum of Sir Barnaby's.'

Corrie was thoughtful. 'Staying in a cosmopolitan hotel like the Now to Zen makes you appreciate the diversity of people, don't you think?'

'No.' Jack was adamant. 'It makes me appreciate being at home among my *non-diverse* friends and loved ones. Particularly those who stuck by me. That's when you find out who really cares about you.'

Corrie nodded agreement. 'Take Tim and Mim, for example. Most of the time they fought like cat and dog, but as soon as either of them was in danger, it was a different story. He was ready to risk his life, going back into the hotel to get Mim out. And when Mim realized what he'd been through, she was terrified she could so easily have lost him.'

Jack put down the paper. 'So what you're saying is that a good way to refresh an ailing marriage is to nearly get yourself murdered? I'm not sure the relationship counselling brigade would agree with you.'

'No, of course I'm not. You're just being provocative.' She wrinkled her brow, thinking back. 'Mind you, when David was nearly killed — twice — it kick-started his relationship with Rainbow, which was what he'd wanted right from the start, except he didn't know it.'

'So how come you knew it?'

'I just did. And another thing. If Louis and Abbie aren't engaged by the end of the year, I'll eat my own cooking.'

'OK, Mystic Meg. What's your prediction for Kelly-Anne?'

'She'll *malaprop* her way through life until some lovely chap scoops her up and surrounds her with babies. She'll wear pretty aprons, daisy chains in her hair and live happily ever after, like in fairy tales.'

'That's a very predictable prediction, if I may say so. You've just made her into a stereotype.'

'Some people like being stereotypes. Take Fred and Rita. It's my guess that they've been stereotypes all their married life and they've had forty wonderfully happy years together. Not everybody wants to be a rampant nonconformist just for the sake of it, you know. It can be very tiring.'

Jack grinned. 'Do you suppose Dorothy Buncombe will find her James Bond stereotype?'

'I shouldn't be at all surprised.' Corrie raised an eyebrow. 'She even had her eye on you for a while.'

'Phew! Now that *would* have been tiring.' Jack was relieved that she hadn't actually made any advances beyond flirtatious smiles. He never knew how to cope in those situations.

'What do you fancy for supper?' asked Corrie.

'Anything but corned beef hash. Funnily enough, I've gone right off it. How about some chips, my little pota-to-peeling-person? And maybe a pizza. I think I'd like some *stereotypical* junk food.'

'I wonder,' mused Corrie, 'if we'll get an invitation to the wedding?'

'Whose wedding?'

'Louis and Abbie's.'

'Aren't you jumping the gun rather?' Jack asked. 'The poor girl's still recovering from the last attempt.'

'I know, but she did say we'd be welcome at the Californian Now to Zen for a vacation. It would be a marvellous holiday — just what we need after the exhausting Brightsea experience. What do you think? Jack! . . . *Jack!* . . . *Come back!*'

THE END

Thank you for reading this book.

If you enjoyed it please leave feedback on Amazon or Goodreads, and if there is anything we missed or you have a question about, then please get in touch. We appreciate you choosing our book.

Founded in 2014 in Shoreditch, London, we at Joffe Books pride ourselves on our history of innovative publishing. We were thrilled to be shortlisted for Independent Publisher of the Year at the British Book Awards.

www.joffebooks.com

We're very grateful to eagle-eyed readers who take the time to contact us. Please send any errors you find to corrections@joffebooks.com. We'll get them fixed ASAP.

Printed in Great Britain
by Amazon